# I don't want to be a Movie Star

## MARGARET PINDER

WALKER BOOKS
AND SUBSIDIARIES

LONDON · BOSTON · SYDNEY · AUCKLAND

LOCATION: PALM DESERT, CALIFORNIA, USA
TIME: DOES IT MATTER?

It was a perfect night: soft, silent and full of stars.

I stood on the balcony looking down into the glistening blue-green depths of the swimming pool below and groaned. If I jumped now, I might just land in the cool, clear water. Just. Then again, I might just break my leg. Maybe that would get me out of here. Not out of here as in "home" perhaps, but out of here, and that had to be a good thing.

Something was moving about below. Or someone. I heard the click of heels on the terrace. Oh great! With just the two of us in the house, there was only one person that could be. But it was 3 a.m.! Couldn't a girl enjoy a good bout of homesickness and major jetlag without the place filling up with extras? I took a hasty step back from the rail hoping to reverse silently the way I had come, but it was too late. A figure had already appeared on the tiles beside the pool and was looking up at me, her face greeny-white in the reflection off the water. I recognized her at once. You would have done too, or you should have, if you knew anything worth knowing about movie history. That face. It was

5

unmistakeable. It was the face of Noni Waters.

Fabulous, beautiful Noni Waters.

Two-time Oscar winner.

Legend.

Goddess.

Diva.

The ultimate movie star.

Maybe to you.

To me: Grandma.

Nightmare.

Witch.

And I was pretty sure she was drunk.

"Katriona?" she warbled. "Is that you?"

Well, duh! Who did it look like? An extra from some low budget sci-fi horror flick?

"No," I called back. "I'm a mutant zombie alien."

She cupped a hand to her ear.

"What was that, darling?"

"Jetlag," I said.

"Poor baby," she cooed.

And, as if on cue, an unbelievably, ridiculously, impossibly small white dog appeared at her side and looked up at me too.

"Poor baby," Noni said again and picked up the dog.

OK, for a minute there I thought she meant me.

"I feel like a zombie," I said.

The dog made a noise that sounded unpleasantly like a snigger and licked my grandmother's chin.

"Would you like to come down and keep me company, darling? While I have a little drinky by the pool?"

I looked at the pool again and tried to judge the distance. Maybe I could just do it. I clenched my fists and closed my eyes. But the madness passed. After all, there is only so much insanity you can blame on jetlag, and this was not exactly a good time for taking a performance dive into several acres of high-finish ceramic edging.

I looked down at my grandmother and tried to think of something sensible.

"I'll be right down," I called.

It was all so wrong.

And although I didn't know it at the time, over the next few days it was going to get a whole lot worse.

Confused? I don't blame you.

OK, let's go back a few reels.

LOCATION: MY KITCHEN, 24 DYSTAPH GARDENS, NORTH OXFORD, OXFORDSHIRE, UK
TIME: ABOUT FIVE WEEKS EARLIER

The first inkling I'd had that something was wrong was the day I got home from school to find my mom gone and my dad in the kitchen slinging pans into a heap in the middle of the floor. Normally this wouldn't bother me, because my dad is the one who does all the cooking in our house anyway. My mom can normally only be persuaded to go anywhere near the oven if Dad is away or, possibly, if somebody's holding a gun to her head.

"Kat! There you are!"

I could tell just looking at him that things weren't good.

"Hi! What's up?"

Mistake! I normally operate a strict "don't ask, don't tell" policy, but there was something about him that threw me off my guard.

He waved a pan at me. It was a Le Creuset. I was impressed. Those things weigh a ton. If I tried that, I'd break my wrist.

"I've just been on the phone to Noni."

Noni? My dad was talking to Noni? OK, that explained a lot. Five minutes on the phone to what must be the mother-in-law from hell would be enough to make any right-thinking man start hurling casseroles at the wall.

"And I saw a mouse. At least I think I saw a mouse. It ran across the floor while we were on the phone. I think it ran into the pan cupboard."

I tried to figure out which was worse: the mouse sighting or the Noni conversation.

"And I made the mistake of shouting at it, then I had to explain to her what was wrong, and when she knew it was a mouse she had a fit. I mean, she's five thousand miles away from the beastly thing, for Christ's sake!"

So?

"Where's Mom?" I said.

I mean, wasn't it her job to deal with Noni?

He began to look a little wild. He still hadn't taken his eyes off the cupboard.

"Where's Einstein?" he said.

"He's asleep on the piano. But..."

"Go and get him and put him in the cupboard."

"But..."

"Just do it!"

I knew not to argue. I went and got Einstein. He complained slightly as I picked him up, but barely opened his eyes as I kissed his furry grey head. He complained a whole lot more when he found himself suddenly being thrust into a cupboard full of pans and the door closed behind him. There was a moment's stunned silence. My dad put his foot against the door. Then the crashing began. We never found out if he got wind of the mouse, but if he didn't, the noise alone would have frightened it away. When the cacophony had subsided to the odd rattle and indignant squawk, Dad opened the door again. Einstein shot out with a wail like a soul in torment and took off out of the kitchen and up the stairs. An avalanche of pans slid out of the cupboard onto the floor. Dad looked inside.

"There," he said. "That sorted that."

Good. It was nice to have closure. Now that the mouse incident had been dealt with satisfactorily, perhaps we could return to more pressing matters.

"Where's Mom?" I asked again.

My dad ran a hand through his hair.

"Ah, yes," he said, and looked at his watch. "She should be at Heathrow by now."

"Heathrow?"

As in the airport, Heathrow?

"Yes," he said. "Sheila called. Your grandfather's had an accident. Fell off a ladder. Silly old coot was trying to spray a wasps' nest under the eaves. He's in hospital now. He's OK, but they think he may have busted his hip. Your mum took the first flight she could get."

I was so shocked that for a moment I didn't know what to say.

"That's one of the reasons I was on the phone to Noni." Now he looked at me properly for the first time since I'd walked in. "The fact is, your mum and I are due at that conference in Georgia this summer. And your grandfather's not going to be well enough to look after you."

My mind was too focused on Grandpa Zack to pick up on the implications of what he'd just said. His next words spelled it out for me.

"You'll have to go to Noni's."

I stared at him.

"Noni's?" I said. "Are you crazy?"

He had the good grace to look uncomfortable.

"I'm sorry," he said. "She called when we were right in the middle of the whole thing and we told her what had happened. She said she would love to have you."

"She did? Why? What's happened to her – has she gone and had a personality transplant along with the Botox?"

The phone rang. My dad leapt as if he'd been stung.

"That could be your mother," he yipped. "I'll take it upstairs."

As he headed for the door he called over his shoulder, "Would you put the pans back for me, hon? Thanks!"

As I knelt on the kitchen floor trying to figure out how to get what looked like two hundred pans back into a space clearly designed to take a maximum of ten, I heard Einstein come back in and sit down expectantly by his food dish.

"You should be doing this," I said. "Not me."

He yawned.

"It's OK for you," I said. "You don't have grand-parents."

He blinked. Einstein may be stupid, but sometimes I think he has the right idea when it comes to disaster: eat and sleep. I slung a copper sauté pan into a corner and tried worrying about Grandpa Zack instead.

By the way, did I mention Einstein is my cat?

This may be a good time to introduce myself: I'm Katriona Shaw, known to all who truly love me as Kat.

10

My grandmother, whose first name I share, prefers the full "Katriona", which is a nerve considering she refuses to answer to anything except "Noni". "Grandma" is a major no-no.

You wouldn't think to look at me that I have movie star genes. Me – the girl with no boobs. I'm fifteen years old, 163 cm tall (that's 5 ft 5 in when I'm in the US) and weigh in at a mighty 47 kg (or 103 lbs, which sounds better, but looks just as bad). Not a gram of which is wasted in the chest department. But I guess we all have our cross to bear, except I seem to have a bigger one than most, which brings me back to Noni and that whole movie-star-genes thing.

You see, just because I'm named after her means everyone likes to pretend I'm just like her. Which would be great if it were true because, even at sixty-two, Noni is still beautiful. I'm not. And if you want to talk about star quality, Noni has it in spades. I don't. What on her is delicate, like a kitten, on me just looks like a scrawny alley cat. She even has those slanty kitten eyes. So do I, but all they do for me is make me look like I have a terminal squint. She has cheekbones; I just have bones. And she has boobs.

I rest my case.

Another major difference between us is that, as you should now be aware, she lives in Palm Desert, California, USA, while I live in Oxford, in the county of Oxfordshire, in Merry Olde England. That normally puts about five thousand miles between us, which is fine by me. I call it the comfort zone.

Not that I don't like California. I mean, what's not to like? But to live…? Especially if you're me (which, obviously, you're not). You see, California isn't really my style. I don't go for all that fluff and tan. My style is skater-dude, mosher-funk, grunge-queen. Not cheer-leader. Not Barbie. Not Miss California. The fluffiest thing in my life is my cat. I do baggy; I do jeans; I do trainers. I do not do skirts; I do not do heels – of any description. I leave my hair, which is straight and dark, to grow pretty much as nature intended, and my skin is so pale my mom force-feeds me iron tablets (when she remembers). Add some fun black eye-pencil and there you have me. Yo!

But enough about me. Time to get back to the story.

Story? Make that "tragedy".

The Tragedy of Katriona Shaw.

LOCATION: PALM DESERT, CALIFORNIA
TIME: GETTING ON FOR 3.15 A.M.

As I stepped back inside my room, I automatically looked for something to put round my shoulders, before remembering that, although it may be the middle of the night, it was also the middle of the summer in the middle of the desert, and consequently plenty warm enough for the T-shirt I was already wearing.

By the time I got downstairs and walked out onto the terrace, Noni had already tottered over to the pool and stretched herself out on one of the loungers. The small white dog, looking unpleasantly like an overgrown rat, had jumped up beside her and snuggled herself into a ball. She pricked an ear as I crossed over to join them, my bare feet making tiny kissing noises on the tile. Noni opened an eye and smiled up at me. She looked lovely. Really. It was almost impossible to believe she was in her sixties. (Or that she was probably tanked to the eyelids.) And her voice was so soft and sweet you would have thought you were talking to

12

a much younger woman. Even without the hats and cunningly wrapped scarves and monster sunglasses she favoured whenever there was a chance she might be spotted in public, her face was smooth and unlined. Amazing. It made me feel like something from the swamp. OK, ten hours on a plane from London to LA hadn't exactly done me any favours in the overall well-being and appearance department, but next to Noni I must have looked a fright.

"Darling," she said, and held up her arms. I wondered briefly what she wanted me to do. Haul her up and toss her into the pool? Unlikely. I bent over and allowed myself to be kissed. Her lips were soft and warm, and she smelled of something sweet and exotic, like jasmine or gardenia.

"Sit down," she said and reached over to pat the lounger beside her. "Unless you want to help yourself to a drink first. Like a Coke or a juice, something like that," she added quickly, presumably in case I got the idea of sneaking something alcoholic and reducing her supplies.

"I'm fine, thanks," I said. I noticed she had something clear and ice-ridden in a frosted glass on the table at her elbow.

"I'm sorry you can't sleep," she said. "I hope you're not an insomniac, like me. I suffer terribly from sleep-lessness."

She turned her lovely head to look at me and pushed out a high-wattage smile. Then she reached out and squeezed my hand. Yeesh!

"It's so lovely to have you here, darling," she said. "It's been far, far too long, don't you think?"

"Oh, absolutely, Noni!"

Liar liar. I could almost smell my panties smoking.

She gave a girlish chirrup of liquid amusement. I tried chirruping back, but it came out as more of a gurgle.

"We'll have such a marvellous time together, we two girls. We'll have to think up lots of fun things to do."

Here, in Palm Desert? With a cast of two? Like what? Spot the cactus? Count the gin bottles? Join the age spots?

"What sort of things do you like? I'm sure fifteen-year-old girls can't have changed all that much since my day."

Don't you believe it, lady. Evolution happens. I decided to illustrate this for her.

"I like skateboarding."

Her chuckle this time sounded like gin over ice.

"Skateboarding? Of course, there was that strange looking thing you brought with you. I did wonder why. But, well, really, you don't expect me to do that, do you!"

"Why not? You might like it."

"Ha ha!"

Glug glug. I was sure I could smell gin on her breath.

"I'd probably break my leg!"

That would be too much to hope for. If Noni broke her leg, I couldn't possibly stay with her. It was a new and interesting twist on my earlier fantasy of hurling myself off the balcony.

"Would it be possible to go to LA at all?"

"Oh darling, you know I hardly ever go out much now."

I didn't, but I might have guessed.

"Besides, we have everything we want right here. You do still swim, don't you dear? The pool is just lovely, especially in this heat."

Ah yes, the pool! No denying that the pool was

something else. OK, the pool was good. Something I could be genuinely enthusiastic about. I looked at it glowing eerily with underwater light.

"Oh yes! The pool is great!"

She seemed to feel this answered all my needs.

"And it is so perfect here. Don't you think?"

I lay back on the lounger and stared glumly upwards. Perfect? Hardly, but there was no denying the fact, as a piece of real estate, yes, it certainly was beautiful. The house itself was unbelievably gorgeous – long and low, a vision of white walls and long stretches of glass which reflected the turquoise sparkle of the illuminated pool. And I had forgotten just how clear the air is in the desert, not to mention the sky. There were so many stars above me it looked as if the whole of the galaxy had heard there was a great intergalactic party over Palm Desert and come along to check out the fun. Big stars, little stars. Whole constellations boogieing away over the humped shadows of the mountains all around. And the air. Oh my, how could air smell so good? I closed my eyes and simply breathed. Yummy yum yum. Even better than chocolate. And, coming from me, that was some praise. What a shame the only person here to enjoy it with me was a sixty-two-year-old recluse with a drink problem.

Something stirred at my elbow. Noni was poking at the ice in her glass with some kind of jewelled prong. Then she was off again.

"Now, darling. It's been so long since I saw you last, you must tell me everything you've been up to. What about school? Have you met any nice boys yet?"

Typical. She couldn't even remember I went to an all-girls' school. I decided to stay off the boy question. I doubt there was anything I could tell a six-times-married film star that would interest her. At least nothing that was true. I decided to keep it clean. I told her about the school play.

"My year did *Twelfth Night* this term, as the end of year play. I was in it. You remember?"

She didn't seem too impressed.

"Oh, the school play," she said, with what sounded just a little like a sneer on the "school" part of it. "Do tell me all about it."

And I swear I heard her yawn. Which would have done wonders for my confidence except I didn't have any anyway, so that was OK.

The trouble is, Noni herself has actually done some "real" acting. By which I mean theatre work. Shakespeare even. There aren't many film stars of her generation, or any generation for that matter, who can say that. Apparently she was good, too. The woman has – had – real talent. Did I mention she won an Oscar twice?

But she was still wittering on.

"Of course, I think it's a mistake to try Shakespeare at your age. You need a certain maturity. Even for the comedies, but especially for the tragedies. Comedy is so hard to pull off. I never played *Twelfth Night*. But I did make a wonderful Beatrice, if I say so myself. *Much Ado About Nothing*, you know. What did you say your part was?"

"My part? Er ... Andrew Aguecheek."

OK, you may laugh, but it is a girls' school, remember. I had wanted to play Feste, but instead I got picked for Sir Andrew. So I had to pretend I was a skinny, romantically frustrated idiot with no boobs. Great. Not that I'd been typecast or anything. Actually, it was kind of a fun part, and as I can't sing that well, it

16

was probably a good thing I wasn't doing Feste. Instead I got to amble around in wrinkly tights looking limp and saying lines like, "I was adored once." If only it were true! I had actually told her all this already in one of our mercifully infrequent phone calls at the time. Was the short-term memory finally going?

She seemed to be digesting the information. Maybe she was just yawning. Again.

"Aguecheek? Really? Well, I expect you managed. You must have inherited some of the Waters genes."

She probably meant it to sound encouraging. Instead she sounded terminally bored. I clenched my fists at my sides and closed my eyes. The woman was too much. She had looks, she had talent and she had boobs. OK, so she was an obnoxious old bat, but she didn't know that or, if she did, it didn't seem to worry her. Life was so unfair. I mean, why couldn't she be the one who fell off the ladder, and not Grandpa Zack? I was going to have weeks of this. I revised my estimate of how quickly I would go mad: two days and I'd be sticking straws in my hair; one week max and I'd be getting cosy in a straitjacket and a padded cell. Oh well, I could always blame it on my genes.

With which happy thought I fell asleep again at last.

LOCATION: PALM DESERT, POOLSIDE EXTERIOR
TIME: LATE MORNING (I THINK)

It was light. I mean, really light. Not light like you get in England, even in the height of summer, but brilliant, brilliant light. Southern California light. Desert light. I was still lying on the lounger, but some kind soul had covered me with what looked like a sarong and opened one of the big poolside umbrellas to shade me from the sun. I struggled upright and looked around.

A woman was walking towards me from the house. Not Noni. I recognized her as Sara, the housekeeper, who I'd met the night before when I'd arrived from LA. She was carrying a tray. A tray? That was promising. Tray usually = food! As she rounded the end of the pool, I spotted a glass and several plates. Excellent. Food it was. Sara smiled to see me awake. I grinned madly at the tray.

"Good morning!"

She had a pleasant, slightly sing-song voice, the kind you imagine doctors using when dealing with the criminally insane. I expect she'd developed it to cope with Noni.

"I brought you something to eat."

I made grateful noises and tried not to look too desperately ravenous.

"It's eleven o'clock already."

Eleven o'clock! No wonder I was hungry.

"Was I out here all night?" I said.

She shrugged and set the tray on a table under the umbrella.

"Esteban came out to check on you before he turned in. He wanted to make sure you wouldn't get cold."

Ah. Esteban – the Hispanic-looking dude with cowboy boots to die for and a neat line in ear jewellery who had collected me from the airport. I guessed he was Noni's driver. I'd liked the look of him. Maybe it was because he had winked at me when he took my bags, but let me keep my skateboard. (A girl should always carry her own skateboard.)

"Thanks," I said. "This looks great."

"If you want, I could make you pancakes, but I thought it was too close to lunch."

Tempt me not! I hesitated to break it to her that I could easily demolish a pile of pancakes and head straight into a three-course lunch without even breaking a sweat.

"Where's Noni? I hope she doesn't mind my sleeping this long."

"She won't. Anyway, she's with Monsieur Alexander right now."

Monsieur Alexander?

Sara must have seen the expression on my face.

"He does her hair and her face," she said matter-of-factly. As if having some weirdo with an unbelievable name come to your house to work his magic were perfectly normal. Whenever I want a haircut, which is about once every few months, I fight my way into the centre of Oxford and get Kerry-Ann, a friendly scissor-wielder of the Gothic persuasion, to whack a few inches off the bottom and send me on my way smelling of jojoba or something equally unpronounceable, but looking more or less the same.

"He's her beauty consultant," she added for good measure.

Beauty consultant. I must try that one out on Kerry-Ann next time the Katriona Shaw fright wig needed another trim.

"He usually comes twice a week, on Mondays and Fridays, but she's expecting Mr Schneider any day now, which is why she's been calling Monsieur Alexander in more regularly."

Monsieur Alexander. Mr Schneider. The household was beginning to sound like the line-up from some European art movie.

Sara unfolded a linen napkin and handed it to me.

"Excuse me, but I have to get on now," she said.

"You take your time. If you need anything, I'll be in the kitchen. I noticed you haven't unpacked yet. If you need any help with that later, just give me a call."

"Thanks," I said. Help with unpacking I did not need. Girl opens suitcase. Girl removes things from suitcase. Girl puts things in cupboards and drawers. Even I could manage that.

As Sara was turning to go back to the house she paused.

"Oh yes," she said. "Your grandfather called about half an hour ago. I told him you were asleep. He said he would call back later."

"Grandpa Zack? Did he say anything else?"

"No, just that he would call back."

Grandpa Zack had called – a voice of sanity from the outside world. And I would be speaking to him soon. At last, something to look forward to! I turned my attention to the food with a new sense of purpose.

Grandpa Zack called just as I had emerged from the sixteen-acre marble bathroom that constituted the ensuite facilities in my room and was putting the final touches to my hair (which, in my world, a world bereft of the likes of Monsieur Alexander, meant giving it a few good swipes with the hairbrush).

The phone by the bed rang and various lights began to flash on the handset. I went over and picked it up.

"Hello?" I said, not too sure I should have answered it.

It was Sara.

"I have your grandfather on the line from Massachusetts," she said. "If you press the green button you'll be able to talk to him."

I inspected the flashing lights, found a green one and

pressed it. Sara disappeared and suddenly I could hear Grandpa Zack shouting down the line.

"Hello! Hello! Goddammit! Is there anyone there!"

I held the phone a little way from my ear and shouted back.

"It's me, Kat! Stop shouting. I can hear you."

"Kat?"

The volume had definitely dropped off. Deeming it safe, I held the phone closer.

"Hi there, Grandpa. How you doing?"

"Hey there, beautiful!" he said. "I'm doing just great, and how's my favourite granddaughter?"

I'm his only granddaughter so that's kind of a joke between us.

"I'm OK," I said.

"Only OK? You don't sound it!"

Am I that obvious?

"What's up?"

"Oh, you know, I'm worried about you and I miss you and I'm going to miss seeing you this summer."

"Oh that!" He was trying to make it sound like no big deal.

"I see you every summer!"

"Well, honey, this summer is going to have to be a bit different."

"You can say that again!"

"Whoa! What's you're problem? You don't want to be spending time with an old man who can't even get out of bed to walk the dog."

"I do so!" I said. "Surely you'll be heaps better soon."

Like that was going to help me now.

He chuckled.

"These things take time. You can't stick a metal pin

in an old man's hip and expect him to go frisking around a few days later."

"What about Spud?"

"Oh Spud will do fine! I've got every kid in the neighbourhood lining up to walk Spud. I think I'm going to have to draw up a roster."

The thought nearly made me want to cry.

"That's my job!" I almost shouted, but there was a funny snuffling woofling noise on the phone so I guess he didn't hear that last bit. He came back on.

"That was Spud saying 'Hi!'"

"Give him a hug from me, will you?"

More rustling and barking, then he was back on the line.

"How are you and Noni getting along?"

I groaned.

"OK, I guess, but ... I don't know. It's just her and me and ... well, there's nothing to do here."

He started laughing.

"Sure, there is," he said. "I'll bet there's heaps to do. And anyway, she is your grandma and she loves you. It's about time she had a turn looking after you."

I must have made some noise of disagreement at this point. I think it may have been a snort.

"Hey, chicken," he said. "Come on. Do the old girl a favour. She needs some human contact, a little slice of the real world and a little reminder that she does have a family and it ain't such a bad one when all's said and done."

That's what I don't get about him. Grandpa Zack was husband number two until Noni dumped him big time and left him with Mom, and instead of hating her guts and being angry with her, he always behaves like she's this kind of amusing old family friend instead of some egomaniac saddo with an image problem.

"You'll get on just fine, Kat. And you can always call me. Just don't stand any nonsense from her. I never did."

"Yeah, and look where that got you."

He chuckled again.

There was one last thing.

"Oh, and Grandpa..."

"That's me."

"I think she's drinking again."

Now there was a pause. When he spoke again the fun had gone out of his voice.

"Is she, now? Well, let's hope not. All the more reason for you not to stand any nonsense."

"Fine," I said, trying not to sound too bitter. "But don't be surprised if I turn up on your doorstep anyway. Then what will you do? With your hip in a sling, you won't be able to chase me away."

He laughed.

"I'll get Spud to do it. He'll chase you all the way back to Palm Desert and bite your butt when you get there."

"He can bite Noni's butt instead," I said, cheering up a little. Thinking about Spud always cheers me up.

"Nah," said Grandpa. "He likes his meat young and sweet. He ain't going to bite a tough old bird like Noni when there's spring chicken like you."

I guess this would be a good point to fill you in on some more of my bizarre family background. Both my parents work at the university: Oxford University. My mom's a physicist and my dad's an economist. My dad's parents, my other grandparents, have been happily married for a gazillion years and live in London, and they're perfectly normal in that understated, totally loopy, British kind of a way. Noni and Grandpa Zack are my mom's mom and dad. NB "mom" not "mum" – yes, if you hadn't spotted it by now, I'm American. But what is super cool is that I'm British too. Two passports. Double happiness. Whichever way I travel between England and the US I get to stand in the shortest line.

Apparently, when my mom told Noni she wanted to be a scientist, she hardly spoke for the rest of the day and then finally asked her if she couldn't think of anything a little more *feminine* to do with her life. That's good coming from Noni. She may have feminine down to a fine art, but underneath she's as tough as old slingbacks. Given her record in the martini drinking stakes, that would be a good nickname for her: "The Old Slingback". Mom and I also lack Noni's man-killer factor. OK, so Noni has had a forty-seven-year head start, but still … I have no boyfriend. I never have. To tell you the truth, I've never even kissed a boy. Not properly, anyhow. And the way things are going, it doesn't look like I'll be breaking my no-snogging record anytime soon. Noni, by contrast, rips through husbands like Kleenex. The last lucky guy, Mr Noni number six, lasted only eighteen months. He was a banker, or something boring like that. The divorce came through three months ago, and two weeks later he dropped dead of a heart attack. Maybe it was delayed shock. I can hardly even remember his name – Karl something. With Noni they never seem to stick around long enough to make it worth the effort. Grandpa Zack lasted the longest, at twelve years, and Mom reckons Noni's still secretly in love with him. But then, she would.

There are a few more characters you ought to know about, but either they haven't put in an appearance yet and you'll meet them when the time comes, or they're back in Oxford and only have walk-on parts for now. The principal of these is my friend Sadie, style-queen and fellow sufferer at the North Oxford High School for Girls (known affectionately to the local townies as the Virgin Megastore). When I found out I was being shipped out to Noni she was the first person I confided in.

LOCATION: COFFEE SHOP INTERIOR, JERICHO, OXFORD, ENGLAND (NO, I HADN'T FOUND A WAY TO FLEE THE COUNTRY AND SEEK REFUGE IN THE MIDDLE EAST)
TIME: ABOUT FIVE WEEKS AGO

Sadie didn't seem to see what the problem was.

"Yeah, but it's California," she said. "How bad can that be?"

Sometimes Sadie lacks imagination.

"Sadie, you benighted trull," I explained, patient as ever. "It might as well be Alaska. I'm going to be doing time with a mad old bint in the middle of nowhere. It's not even LA; it's the desert. There's nothing to do."

"Doesn't she have servants and stuff?"

For Sadie this represents the peak of good living. Actually Sadie's parents wait on her hand and foot, but even they draw a line at cleaning her room; she needs a maid.

"Sure she does. But servants aren't the same as like-minded friends. Friends my age, or within fifty years of my age, that is."

"Well, won't you be able to get away to LA sometimes? How far is it, anyway?"

"A hundred and ten to a hundred and twenty miles."
(Which is nothing by American standards, virtually
next door.) "That's not the point. I'm being sent out to
stay with a woman I barely know. And what I do know
about her, I don't like much. What am I going to do?
My parents seem to think she's upset about ex-husband
number six. Sorry, make that terminally-ex, ex-husband
number six. And they want me to keep an eye on her
drinking. I'm being sent out there as some kind of grief
counsellor. And minder. When I'm not holding her
wrinkled claw and telling her she's bound to meet Mr
Right number seven any day now, I'll be searching the
premises for hard liquor and pouring it down the sink.
It's going to be a full-time job."

"Can't you go and hang out in the neighbourhood?
That way, you might meet some cool guys."

"You simply don't get it, do you, girl? There is no
neighbourhood. They don't live like that out there.
They haven't worked their wrinkly butts off to make
their pile and retire to a dream home in Palm
Wherever to find themselves back in a "neighbourhood". If she has neighbours, they all live miles away,
and they're all just as old and mad as she is. It would-
n't even be worth the walk. At least if I were sixteen, I
could drive."

"Except you have to be sixteen."

Sadie has an unhappy knack of stating the obvious.

"Which you're not."

See?

"Maybe you should let her get drunk from time to
time and make a run for it."

OK, it was an option. Not a very attractive option,
but at least it would give me something to cling to
until I could come up with something better.

26

There's one other person you maybe ought to know about. It's a guy. A cute guy. But I'm not too sure what to tell you about him. Or if I want to talk about him at all. Leave it with me. I may come back to him.

But don't hold your breath.

After I'd showered and made myself presentable – presentable by my definition, not Noni's, i.e. jeans and a red Che Guevara T-shirt, zero make-up – I ambled downstairs to see if Noni had been returned to human society (mine). Apparently she hadn't, so I decided to take a quick tour of the premises to remind myself where everything was. It had been a while since I was last here. I headed to the back of the house and the kitchen, but Sara wasn't there any more, so I went out the back door to look around.

There was a large powder blue Cadillac parked by the garage. Mind you, when did you ever see a small Cadillac, powder blue or otherwise? They only seem to come in two sizes: extra-large and monster. This one looked a bit of a vintage model. Some fun chrome touches. Cute.

I grinned at it to show my approval and set off at a brisk trot round the side of the house. And immediately collided with a wall. At least I thought it was a wall until it took a step back and said, "Steady on, love!" in one of the broadest Northern accents I've heard outside *Coronation Street*. I squinted up at the source of the vowels (yeesh, but that sun was bright) and vaguely made out a huge man-shaped object topped with a spiky thatch of ginger hair.

27

"Sorry!" I said. "I didn't see you."

Gazing into the sun like that, I still couldn't.

A ham-like hand touched my shoulder and guided me back round the corner and into the shade. *Now* I could see him. He was what is known in girl-speak as "very big man". He was wearing a Hawaiian shirt covered in a pattern of surfers and hibiscus so bright it made his massively freckled face and ginger curls look positively pale.

He smiled down at me. I swallowed hard. Isn't that what giants always do before they go into the whole "fee fo fi fum" routine and start planning lunch with you as the main feature on the menu?

"I'm sorry," I said again. Not very original, but then, "Please, Mr Giant, don't eat me" would have sounded wet.

"No problem, love," he said, then he did an odd thing. He pinched my chin gently between his thumb and forefinger and tilted my face up and ... well, just looked at it. Not at me. At my face. Was he planning the best place to take a bite? I could hear my inner hamster screaming "No-o-o-o!" Then he nodded as if satisfied and said, "Do you use sun block?"

Typical bloody desert dweller. I decided to humour him.

"Not usually," I said.

"You should," he said. "Every day. And I mean every day. Sun damage to skin starts early."

Cheek! I felt like saying, "What? You mean I could end up getting a million ugly freckles like yours?"

Not that I mind freckles, but his were way over the top.

I just gurgled instead.

He let go of my chin. Now he seemed amused. Big git.

"I was looking for my grandmother," I said, a little haughtily.

"Oh, aye?" he said. That voice! It was unreal. He sounded like he'd wandered off the set of *Wuthering Heights*. "She's round by the pool." Or maybe it was "She's round by t'pool." They can be subtle, these Northern types.

The landscape shifted sideways. Not an earthquake. Just Man Mountain stepping round me. Heathcliff on steroids.

Round by t'pool, eh?

"Thanks!" I called after him as he lumbered down the drive, remembering my manners at last.

He raised a hand the size of Chicago and waved without looking round.

I found the pool and there, stretched out on a pink lounger beneath a huge umbrella at the far side as if she'd never left, was Noni.

I tootled round to her obediently. She held up her arms and cooed, "Darling! I thought you were never going to wake up."

No, I didn't seize this new opportunity and yank her poolwards, but leaned down dutifully and pecked her not-so-very-wrinkled cheek. Surprisingly, although she was out in broad daylight, she had shunned the bee-keeper veils in favour of an enormous hat, which could have seated most of King Arthur's knights, and sun-glasses to match. She patted the lounger cushion beside her and invited me to sit down. Invited me? I know an order when I hear one. I sat.

"Did you sleep well?"

"Did I ever," I said. "I must have fallen asleep while we were talking. I'm sorry."

She didn't seem to have taken offence. Maybe she didn't always need an audience – not a conscious one, anyway. I was about to ask her who the big ginger-haired guy I'd bumped into was, but she was already off warbling about what a wonderful day it was (I thought it was always a wonderful day in Palm Desert – isn't that what they paid for?), and would I like to swim? Actually, that sounded like a great idea. My T-shirt was already feeling warm against my skin. I remembered the ginger giant's Hawaiian shirt. That had looked pretty cool in an ironic, all-American way. Maybe I should invest in one for myself.

"You did bring a swimsuit, didn't you, dear?"

Of course I had. I noticed she was suited up. Some winsome number in navy, dotted with white bows that echoed the mega-hat. Mine was black. Dotted with black. With black trim. Definitely not winsome.

"You can swim anytime you like," Noni was saying. "But do make sure you wear sun block. Skin like ours needs looking after."

Skin like ours? What a nerve! I looked at her face again. It *was* uncannily youthful. I couldn't quite tell if she was wearing make-up or not. Clever, that. Did I detect the handiwork of Monsieur Alexander or of some fiendishly cunning surgeon (plastic, naturally)? Probably both. I couldn't check out the hair because of the hat. I scanned down. Slim, flat stomach. Tanned legs. Aha! Wrinkly tanned legs with a touch of leather about them. I could see my own ankles peeking mod-estly out from under the hem of my baggy jeans. Very white. Oh, yuck! A touch of the cave-dwelling maggot creature about them.

"Here's Sara with a drink for us."

I turned and saw the long-suffering one emerging

from the glass doors with another tray.

A drink, eh? What did that mean? More juice for me and a tankard of gin for Madame Leather Legs?

Actually, when we went over to sit at the table it turned out to be a pitcher of iced tea. Sara poured, and I didn't see Noni slip anything untoward into hers from some hidden hip flask.

"Cheers!"

Cheers? Maybe the stuff was in there already.

We clinked glasses and I took a cautious sip. Nope, no illicit alcohol-related substances.

Noni lowered her glass.

"Well, darling, it was so nice hearing all your news last night ..."

My news? What news? I didn't remember any news. I was fifteen. I was alive. I was here.

She was still prattling on.

"... but now I have something exciting of my own to tell you about."

That sounded ominous. Probably a likely prospect for her next marital victim. I braced myself for the worst and let her snap right into it.

She came over all coy and looked down into her drink and then over at some fancy bushes covered in purple flowers at the other side of the pool.

"You know I haven't appeared in a movie for a long time now."

I certainly did. But an encouraging "uh huh" seemed in order. I pushed one out and sent it her way.

"Well, I got a call from Jack Winemaker last month. You do know who Jack Winemaker is, don't you, darling?"

I surely did, "darling." Movie trivia was my specialist subject. Another, more enthusiastic "uh huh!"

seemed to satisfy her.

"Jack called. He has a new project he's really excited about and – can you believe this? – he wants me to make a comeback and play one of the leads!"

She was so excited she actually took off her sunglasses so I could see her eyes sparkling. Wow! I could hardly look her in the face, they were so dazzling.

"A new Jack Winemaker project!" she breathed.

I could tell something more than "uh huh" was needed. Besides, I'd pretty much exhausted the potential of that one.

"Oh wow," I said with a forced brightness that struggled to match my grandmother's eyes. "That's so great!"

"Isn't it? I've read the script and it's wonderful! So perceptive."

Perceptive, eh? I wonder what age character they wanted her to play? That would be the acid test on "perceptive".

"So," I said. "What's it about?"

She went all coy again.

"Let's just say it's a celebration of the sexual power of the older woman," she said, and put her sunglasses back on.

I nearly choked on my tea.

The sunglasses turned my way.

"Do you think your mother will mind very much?" she asked, her voice throbbing with faux concern?

Mom? Mind? How was I supposed to know? (Although I expected the answer to that would be a big fat "yes".) And what about me? How did she think I would feel seeing my sixty-two-year-old grandmother flashing her "sexual power" in every cinema in the country?

Somehow neutral grunting didn't seem to cover it any more. Time for that top class Katriona Shaw diplomacy (known to the rest of the world as "lying").

"Noni," I said, my voice throbbing like a lawnmower, "it sounds wonderful."

She pressed a hand to her heart. Or to the place where her heart would have been if she'd had one. Now her face (or what I could see of it) became serious.

"Katriona," she said, solemnly. "You are very wise for your age."

At least one of us was.

"The producer, Sam Schneider, is going to be coming here sometime soon to discuss the project. I hope you'll still be here when he does. It will be nice for you to meet someone like him. Someone who knows me from my earlier days in the movie business. I know I must seem like a silly old thing to you, Katriona, darling." (From your lips to God's ears, lady.) "But, you know, sweetie pie, I was someone once."

I knew! I knew! It didn't help.

I managed a rigid smile.

"You still are, Noni," I said, with all the sincerity I could muster.

History may condemn me, but it seemed the right thing to do at the time.

Nothing happened the rest of the day. And I mean nothing.

At about 2.30 Noni went to her bedroom for a nap. I was feeling pretty tired myself. My body clock was still trying to figure out local time. I thought about having a sleep too, but decided it was probably better to stay awake and try to make myself adapt to the new time zone. So I had a swim instead.

LOCATION: PALM DESERT, THE POOL
TIME: SOMETIME MID-AFTERNOON

I drifted up and down in the pool, feeling the alternating glow of sun and cool water on my skin. This I could get used to, I thought. I floated on my back and looked up into the high blue sky through half-closed eyes and imagined what it must be like to live like this all the time. I tried to feel what it must be like to be Noni. I couldn't. Hardly surprising really. Lathered in sun block, I gave up and simply let myself hang there in the water, eyes closed, enjoying the warmth and quietness and a few private daydreams (e.g. that one day I would have boobs – real ones – or get that first snog).

I guess I must have fallen into a hypnotic doze at this point because the next thing I was aware of was a voice somewhere above and to the left of me making a coughy noise and saying, "Excuse me." I came back to consciousness with a start that made my arms and legs jack-knife in towards my stomach and sent me shooting under the water with a squawk. I bobbed back to the surface spluttering and cursing, and struggled to get the water out of my eyes and my lungs. Not good. I waded to the side of the pool, arms extended in front of me like a zombie from some Fifties B-movie, uttering inhuman cries of distress and clutching at the air. The voice was still there, making what sounded like concerned noises, and as I bumped up against the edge of the pool squinting and gurgling, a towel was placed in my waggling fingers. I buried my face in it and attempted to restore some order to the Katriona Shaw life-support system. After a few seconds of rubbing and

34

moaning it worked, and I was able to lift my head to the source of the voice. I saw… a total god.

Oh yes, make no mistake about it. I was neither asleep nor hallucinating under the influence of too much desert sun and inhaled pool water. The figure now hunkered down on the tiles, exquisite brow furrowed with apparent interest and concern, was the full 24-carat, no holds barred, batteries included GOD. I blinked and gasped, only this time it wasn't because I'd just nearly drowned myself.

"Urgh," I said. Which, unfortunately, is not god-speak for "Hello, you beautiful vision, I worship you and want to have your babies," but just means "urgh".

The god smiled. Oh radiance. Dazzling radiance! "Expensive American orthodontics" I heard a cynical voice whisper at the back of my mind.

The god spoke.

"Hey, there," he said. "I'm sorry. I didn't mean to startle you."

I waved a cheery hand and fought to control my breathing.

"That's OK," I managed. "You didn't really."

Which suggested that I regularly went into convulsions while swimming, just for the hell of it, and he merely happened to chance along in time to witness one of my finest efforts. Bad.

"I mean, you did. A bit. But it doesn't matter."

"Well, I sure am sorry," he said again. "No hard feelings, I hope."

Absolutely not! Powerful, disturbing feelings, maybe, but not hard.

"I was getting out anyway," I said. Not true, but it made conversation, and, since he'd showed up, I could think of any number of good reasons why I should be out of the water and on dry land. Where he was.

"Here, let me help you."

He held out a hand.

Eek! He wanted me to touch him. Eek!

I had a sudden moment's panic that I was "eeking" out loud, but his friendly expression hadn't changed to one of fear and doubt – yet. I took his hand and felt long fingers closing around my wrist and suddenly – whoosh – I was flying up through the water and found myself landing gently on my feet.

"Here." He picked the towel up and draped it round my shoulders. I clutched at it like an elderly aunt surprised in the shower.

"Thank you," I said.

Thank you. Thank you. Thank *you*!

Now I was on more of a level with him, no longer blinded by water and sunlight, and as my main concern had ceased to be where my next breath was coming from, I could look at him properly.

It was worth doing.

He was medium height, tanned a rich, smooth bronze, with straight black hair that brushed his shoulders, black eyes, a straight nose, a dimple in his chin that looked exactly as if someone had fetched him a swift one with a snooker cue, and an interesting line in lips. It was as if some benign maniac had mixed up the best of Hugh Jackman and Johnny Depp, and come up with a kinder, gentler version of both. Just for me. Please God.

"I'm Taylor," he said.

"I'm Kat."

"Nice to meet you, Kat."

And what precisely was Taylor doing here? It didn't seem polite to ask.

"I'm Noni's granddaughter," I offered. Maybe he'd do a trade on the information. "I'm staying here for a few weeks while my parents are in Georgia. That's Georgia as in Russia-Georgia. Not Georgia-Georgia."

Too much information! Stop running off at the mouth. But, OK, maybe it served a purpose. Maybe it was keeping me from drooling too obviously.

He simply nodded.

"I didn't know Miss Waters had a granddaughter."

Obviously my fame had not gone before me. I tried an airy laugh. I was going to say "Sometimes she forgets she has one too," but decided it might not be a good idea until I knew exactly who this Taylor god-person was.

"Yes, she does," I said instead. "I'm afraid I'm it."

He smiled again.

"Nice," he said. But whether he meant nice for me or for Noni, I couldn't tell.

"I do the pool," he said, and jerked his head to indicate a pile of equipment I hadn't spotted, lying by one of the loungers.

Aha! A pool god. So far, so good. Now what?

I looked at the pool for inspiration. It looked blank.

He went over to his stuff and came back with a small box, which he flipped open. It contained a row of glass tubes. He knelt down and scooped some water up in a plastic jug and filled the tubes. Neat.

"I suppose I should leave you to get on," I said, reluctantly.

"You're not bothering me," he said, doing something sexy with the tubes and closing the box.

You're bothering *me*, I thought, watching his thighs bulging into clearly defined muscles as he crouched and stood up.

"So, do you live around here?" I asked, trying to sound casual. Of course nobody really lived within miles of "here" (unless he was a wild man of the desert who made his home with the coyotes) but I figured that around here, "around here" meant a radius of a good twenty miles.

"Kind of."

He *was* coyote man.

"My folks live in Palm Desert. My dad has a pool maintenance business, but I'm at school in LA."

School? Yikes! What kind of hormones was he on? He looked all of twenty-something. Then I remembered that in the States, "school" meant "university" as well.

"You're a college student?"

He was making with a long-handled net now, fishing invisible bits of leaf and unwanted crud off the surface of the pool.

"Yup, I'm doing Fine Art at UCLA."

You see L what? Lucy Olé? YMCA?

I was about to launch into the whole Village People routine when I remembered UCLA stood for University of California, Los Angeles. Sometimes it helps having parents who are academics. Sometimes. So I stopped before I could get as far as raising my arms above my head and do that stupid mime that goes with the chorus. Good. He would probably have thought I was having another convulsion.

He turned the net inside out and flicked a few leaves and blossoms into the bushes.

"But I help my dad out some days."

"That's nice," I said, and meant it. "Do you always do Noni's pool?"

Trying not to sound too eager.

Then I heard Sara calling to me from the doors into the house. It seemed my presence was required. Noni was up and on the prowl.

"I have to go," I said, rather obviously.

"Me too. I'm just about finished up here now."

He smiled a broad and devastating smile. Oh boy, those teeth. I could virtually see stars of light flashing on every incisor.

"I'll be seeing you around, then."

"Er ... yeah ... I hope so."

"Me too."

He picked up his box and shouldered the net. I clutched my towel, trying to cover my unhealthy pallor and lack of boobs, and grinned inanely.

As he left, I went round the pool to where Sara was waiting, trying not to make it too obvious I was watching him out of the corner of my eye.

Suddenly life chez Noni had a bright side.

OK time to talk about boys. Boys in general. And *that* boy. Not Pool God. The other one. The one I think I mentioned before. Maybe it's time he got a walk-on part in the movie. If we're talking boys, then I guess he should. But don't get excited. There's not much to tell.

LOCATION: OXFORD, ENGLAND
TIME: FLASHBACK AROUND SIX WEEKS EARLIER

I was in the park with my regular gang one fine weekend, scooting up and down on my skateboard, practising some new manoeuvres while Sadie watched from the safety of a bench (why risk a broken nail by doing anything more physical than trying to figure out if she looked better crossing her legs at the knee or the ankle?), when one of the lads, Mike – known as Mike the Mattress on account of his powerful body odour – ambled up with a boy I hadn't seen before. He waved to us and we converged on him and upped boards.

"Hi there," said Mike. "This is Jamie. He's going to be moving here this summer, so I brought him along to hang with us today, if that's OK with you guys."

Was it OK? Well, duh!

As I checked out the new arrival I was aware of Sadie rapidly unwrapping her legs and drifting across to join us, trying to look radiant and lovely. Which, as usual, she did. Jamie was definitely worth looking radiant and lovely for. He was about my height, with floppy blond hair (if it really was naturally blond – you never know nowadays) and he had hardly any spots. Unusual in a skater, if our little clique is anything to go by. I don't know why I pegged him as a skater, as he didn't have a board with him, but there was something about him that suggested he was one of us. We said "Hi!" all round and then, just as Sadie's radiant loveliness was getting that bit too blinding and I was feeling suddenly baggy and depressingly boob-free, Mike said Jamie could borrow his board if he wanted, which he did, and he went off with the others to race up and down the path. I joined them, partly because I wanted to skate and partly because I wanted to check him out some more, while Sadie returned to her bench and her leg-crossing exercises. After a bit, still following Jamie out of the corner of my eye, I went and sat back down with her. I saw Jamie give the board back to Mike and stand back to watch the others, so I took a breath to pluck up courage and called out that he could borrow mine if he wanted. I heard Sadie whisper "Nice move" under her breath as he ambled over and took it from me.

As a board it's nothing special, but I did customize it myself with a design of a Celtic dagger against a background of flaming thorns. Jamie turned it over in his hands to look at it.

"This is really cool," he said. "Did you do it?"

He sat down next to me. Not next to Sadie, I noticed. Next to me. Sadie noticed too, and rolled her eyes.

"I did mine with a pentacle and a border of skulls," he said. "I'll bring it to show you next time."

Next time? I saw Sadie prick up her ears, but I think that was at the mention of a pentacle. She's into that whole Wiccan number, except it's all a bit designer-Wicca with her. She claims to be tuning into the Mother Spirit of the Earth or whatever, when she's really trying to find a spell that will make her nose shorter. (Gaia, Gaia, pants on fire.) She is rather hung up on appearance. Like Noni. Thinking about it, I reckoned maybe I should send her out to Palm Desert instead of me. She and Noni would get on like a house on fire. I'd say like two witches on fire, in fact, but that would be in bad taste, so I won't.

We were getting on really well, but then Mike came up and performed some fancy manoeuvre in front of us (failed – the board shot out from under him) and it was time for them to go. I asked Jamie if he was going to be around any more, but he said he had to go back home to somewhere awful like Hull the next day, which was a shame. He seemed kind of disappointed too, which was nice. There was one of those awkward moments when we just stood looking at each other, then Mike started pulling on his sleeve, so he gave this kind of half wave and said "See you around" and I did the same and said "Yeah, I guess you will," and he went off back to the North to eat mud or whatever they do up there. So that was that.

End of story. Not very exciting, I know. But there it is.

CUT TO: PALM DESERT, HOME OF POOL GOD AND, CONSEQUENTLY, A FINER, BETTER PLACE
TIME: LATER THAT DAY

I soon had a new and willing convert to the cult of Pool God – the ever-faithful, ever-nosy Sadie.

I called her that evening from my room. In a rare moment of insight and generosity, Noni had said I could call my friends any time I wanted. Sadie listened in rapt silence to my description of the afternoon's visitation.

"Oh wow!" she breathed. "Was he for real?"

"He certainly was," I said. "A vision, maybe, but solid flesh and blood. His hand felt solid enough."

"His hand?" she squealed. "He touched you?"

She made it sound positively obscene.

"He helped me out of the pool," I said.

"What were you wearing?"

Now that was obscene! If I hadn't known it was Sadie I would have slammed the phone down and called the police to report a heavy breather.

"My black swimsuit."

"Not that one? Not *the* black swimmie?"

As I only had the one, of any colour, I had to assume that was the one she meant.

"Yes. Why?" I said with as much dignity as I could muster. "What's wrong with it?"

A distant sigh rippled up to some satellite over the Atlantic, touched down in North Carolina and vaulted across the continent to my ear. Some sigh.

"There's nothing exactly wrong with it," she said. "That's what's wrong with it."

Dear Sadie: logical to the end.

"Girl, with your figure I don't know why you don't invest in a bikini. Bikinis were designed for women like you."

Bikini bottoms. Maybe. If you go for that "sticks in a bag" look. Bikini tops?

"Sadie," I said, as gently as I could, as if it was her problem and not mine. "You're forgetting I have no boobs."

A pause crouched, ready to do that whole satellite-leaping number then realized, what the hell, it was just a pause anyway, and sat tight.

"It's not that you have *no* boobs," Sadie began at last.

Another pause. She was trying to think of a way to put it tactfully. I knew that, being Sadie, she couldn't. I jumped in quickly to spare myself further pain.

"Meaning? That I have, what, three or something?"

She actually laughed.

"No, you idiot," she said. "Of course you have boobs."

Oh really? Where?

"It's just that if you behave like a girl with no boobs, everyone will think you don't have any."

"I don't need to pretend," I said. "I don't."

"Yes, you do."

"No, I don't."

"You do so."

"I do not so."

This was going nowhere fast. Why was Sadie suddenly so keen to persuade me my chest was not the chest I knew and, if I didn't actually love, I recognized and accepted as my own? A horrible suspicion flashed across what was passing for my mind right then.

"Have you been casting more of your spells again?"

A silence. Aha! Now I had her.

"No!" She sounded cross now. "Look, is there a mirror anywhere near where you are?"

A mirror? The house was riddled with them.

"In the bathroom," I said, suspiciously. "Why?"

"Can you take the phone with you?"

Could I take the phone? Where did she think I was? Intensive care?

"Sure."

"Then go look at yourself in the mirror."

"Why?"

Another sigh.

"Just do it. For me. Do it for your Aunty Sadie."

In the bathroom I looked in the mirror. One skinny creature of the female persuasion stared back sulkily.

"Are you there yet?"

"Yup."

"Are you looking in the mirror?"

"Yup. Haven't spotted any boobs yet, though."

"Turn sideways."

I turned sideways.

"OK."

"Well?"

"No boobs."

"Oh for heaven's sake, Kat. Look!"

I looked.

"Well?"

I was about to repeat myself, but in the spirit of strictest honest I felt compelled to admit to a modest frontal swelling.

"A modest frontal swelling," I said. "But nothing you could actually classify as…"

"Stand up straight!" she ordered.

Yikes! I glanced at the phone for a video-link attachment. How did she do it? Maybe she was a witch. I stopped hunching over and stood up straight.

"Well?"

"I dunno … I…"

"You see."

I did. Kind of.

"OK," I said. "If I stand up straight there may be a suspicion of a bulgette under the old T-shirt."

"Pull your shoulders back."

Oh, for crying out loud!

I pulled my shoulders back.

"And? Does that help?"

"A bit. But I can't go around…"

"There you are, then. I told you so."

She was hopeless.

"Can I stop looking in the mirror now?"

"Yes. But you have to practise walking around with your head up and your shoulders back. Try it now."

I strutted back into the bedroom, head up, chin out. I felt like a pigeon.

"How's that?"

"Fine," I lied, and made pecking noises down the phone.

"What's that kissy noise?"

"Nothing," I said. "And it wasn't supposed to be a kissy noise."

"Well, thank God for that. Now, tell me more about Pool God! D'you think you might be able to send me a picture…?"

I sighed. I'd already told her everything (which

wasn't much). Twice.

At least it had got her off the subject of boobs.

We chatted about the usual pointless things we girlies talk about when we're not stressing about our boobs, and I had the feeling that the conversation (if that's not too grand a word for our aimless ramblings) had just about run its course when Sadie said, "Oh, by the way, that boy was in the park again today."

That boy?

"What boy?" I said, trying not to sound too interested.

"Jamie. The skater. The one who came to the school play..."

"Oh him!" I said quickly. The last thing I wanted to think about was the school play. Not in connection with Jamie anyway. The scars were still too fresh.

There was a pause.

"He asked where you were."

Probably so he could have another good snigger at my expense.

"Did he?" I wanted to say "Wow!" but I kept it to myself. "What did you tell him?"

"I told him where you were, of course."

"What did he say?"

"Nothing, really."

I tried not to feel disappointed. What did I expect? What was there to say other than "Good!" or "Fancy that" (except he obviously didn't)?

"Then he went off with Mike and some of the other guys."

I tried to draw some comfort from the thought that at least Sadie hadn't managed to lure him up to the disaster area that was her room.

There was a pause. Sadie seemed to be awaiting

something more by way of a response.

"Oh," I said feebly. "Er … if you see him again, tell him I said 'Hi!'"

"I will," she said, without any apparent enthusiasm.

Thanks, Sade!

So that was that.

I had only nicely eased Sadie off the phone after extracting a pang-making description of what everyone in the gang was up to (everyone except Jamie, that is) when there was a scratching noise at the door and in trotted the little white rat-dog (whose name, I'd since discovered, was Madge). Now there was a surprise.

"What do you want?" I said, maybe a little more grumpily than I would have done if she hadn't caught me in the middle of another major bout of homesickness. Well, friend-sickness anyway.

She frisked across the floor and sprang up onto the bed. Cheek! She pattered across the covers and sniffed my fingers. I tickled her ears. She closed her eyes with pleasure and made short, wheezing noises. This wasn't so bad.

"What's the matter, old girl?" I said. If I couldn't actually say it to Noni, I could at least try it out on her dog.

Madge opened her eyes again and, I swear to God, rolled them at me.

"Is it Noni?" I said.

The tiny tail wagged briefly. She hopped back down off the bed and ran to the door where she stopped and looked back at me expectantly.

"What?"

She barked.

"Forget it," I said. "I'm going to bed now. Me have

jet lag. Me sleep now."

She barked again.

"OK, OK."

For a rat-dog, she had one hell of an attitude on her. I followed her to the door, grumbling. She grinned. At least that's what it looked like to me. She skittered out onto the landing and bobbed down the wooden stairs, nails clicking on the wood. Down I went after her, across the huge entrance hallway and into the modest room that gave onto the terrace (by "modest" I mean the one with the fountain in the middle of the floor and the fully stocked bar). No Noni. But Madge was already slipping through the glass doors to the terrace and the pool.

Noni was stretched out on the lounger, apparently asleep. I hesitated, not sure what I should do. Madge raised her nose and gave an urgent whimper.

OK, OK. I walked round the pool. She followed me, wagging her tail and jumped up onto a free lounger. I put my hand on her head to quieten her while I looked at Noni. Her head was tilted to one side, her sunglasses askew on her nose. Was she asleep? Dead? Yikes! But no, her chest was rising and falling and I thought I could detect a faint snore. Hmm, attractive, that. But at least she wasn't dribbling. There was one of those cute V-shaped cocktail glasses on the table next to the lounger. I reached out carefully, picked it up and sniffed it. So that was it. I might have known.

"You can put that down as soon as you like, young lady."

Noni.

I nearly dropped the glass in surprise.

"Er ... hello," I said, and put the glass down. Fast. "I just came to see where you were."

"Well, I'm here."

She didn't sound too pleased to see me.

"Madge came into my room. I thought she was looking for you."

Noni had been regarding me through half-open eyes. Now she opened them a bit wider and struggled to sit up.

"Baby!" she said.

I assumed that didn't mean me.

I assumed correctly. Hearing her mistress's voice, Madge hopped across from her lounger to Noni's side and received a hug and a rather random kiss that landed on the side of her head. She looked up at me with a smirk. I stared her down. What made her think I was jealous of *that*?

There was an awkward silence, and I thought Noni had passed out again. I'm sorry, I meant to say "fallen asleep again". I was debating whether to leave her there, guarded over by the trusty Madge, put her to bed or find something to lay over her, when one eye opened and fixed me with a surprisingly beady stare.

"He didn't come," she said and her voice rang with tragedy. "He said he would come, but he didn't."

"He didn't?"

Now who did she mean?

"Sam didn't come."

Oh, Sam.

*Sam?*

"Sam Schneider?"

"He didn't come."

This was getting a tad repetitive.

"Did he say he was coming today?"

She seemed to consider this, still watching me through one eye.

"No, he didn't. But he said 'soon'."

I couldn't see what the big deal was.

"Why don't you call him?"

Now the other eye snapped open and stared at me with something like disgust.

"Because ..." I realized she was speaking far more carefully than any sober person would. "... because..." She seemed to like the word. She smiled and tried it again. It obviously felt good. "Because *I* don't call people; they call *me*."

Of course.

Now she closed her eyes again, but her free hand suddenly shot out and grabbed my wrist. Ouch!

"Why doesn't he call?" Her voice was like a little girl's. I saw her lip tremble. A single tear crept out of the corner of her eye and slid over her cheek towards her ear. Her grip tightened on my wrist.

What was I supposed to say?

"Don't cry," I said, helplessly. "I expect he's busy. You know what these Hollywood people are like..."

Snore.

Excuse me?

She was snoring. Head back, eyes closed, mouth open. I could almost see the little carpenter sawing wood up her nose. Rasp. Squeak. Her grip on my wrist had not relaxed its pressure. I stood there helplessly, tied to the side of the lounger like some poor dog tethered outside a newsagents.

Oh great. Now what?

"Noni?" I said, hopefully. "Noni!"

Nothing.

I stood looking down at her. But I couldn't just leave her there. Awful warnings about drunken people being left on their backs and drowning in their own puke filled my head. But I couldn't see how I could turn her over without rolling her right off the lounger and straight into the pool, where she could drown the conventional way.

I needed help. Pool God, where are you now?

I sat down on the nearest lounger and looked at her glumly. Madge trotted over and jumped up beside me.

"Now what?" I said, but she seemed to have run out of ideas. A quick look at my watch told me it was probably too late to find Sara.

"I guess I'd better sit here and keep an eye on her," I said to Madge.

She sighed and did that turny-roundy thing dogs do before lying down with her head on her paws. It looked like it was going to be a long night.

LOCATION: PALM DESERT, A LOUNGER BESIDE THE POOL
TIME: LATER – DON'T ASK ME HOW LONG

I must have nodded off, because I woke up suddenly when I felt Madge jump down off the lounger.

Then I heard the footsteps.

It was Esteban.

Madge raced over when she saw him and did a few fast circuits of the boots. He ignored her and nodded to me.

"Hey there," he said. "Isn't it kind of late to be sunbathing?"

Then he saw Noni and stopped. I wished I'd taken the glass inside. It was all rather obvious. He didn't look too surprised.

"Er ... I found Noni ... er ... asleep out here and I thought I ought to stay with her," I said.

"Huh?" he said. "You don't got to do that."

He jerked his head back towards the house.

"There are some blankets over the back of the couch in there," he said, "Maybe you could bring me a couple."

I found them and brought them out to him. He laid one gently over Noni as if she were a sleeping infant, then he stretched himself out on the lounger next to her and draped the other across his legs. He yawned and tucked his hands behind his head.

"You go to bed," he said. "I'll stay here with her. You don't got to worry."

He looked as if he was in for the long haul.

"But you could be here all night."

He shrugged.

"It wouldn't be the first time."

It seemed to amuse him.

"Can I get you anything?"

"Nope. I'll be fine. You go to bed now."

As I went back into the house I looked back. Esteban had tipped his hat over his eyes and crossed one foot over the other at the ankles, which made the pointy toes of his boots stick up like two little tents under the blanket. Madge was curled up on his stomach. As I watched I saw him lay one strong brown hand on her, almost covering her tiny body, and she settled down without a murmur.

I went on up the stairs to bed feeling very, very safe – and even more alone.

LOCATION: PALM DESERT
TIME: AROUND 9 A.M.

If I'd thought Noni was going to make a big deal out of the evening's events next morning, I needn't have worried. As I stepped out into the blinding sun (did it ever rain here?) I was greeted by a merry "Halloo!" with a "darling" thrown in for good measure. And there she was, the Merry Widow herself, in full regalia, seated at the table, bright of eye and bushy of tail. That woman had stamina.

She began talking before I even sat down. I looked at her closely while I pretended to unfold a napkin in my lap. She looked terrific. I know life isn't generally supposed to be fair, but really, this was against nature. It confirmed my sneaking suspicion that, somewhere along the line, Noni had made a pact with the devil. I also suspected that if either one of them ever came to regret it, it wouldn't be Noni.

"Darling! Have some juice. Granola?"

"Thanks."

She reached over and patted my hand. Strange.

"Now, darling, would you like to go out today?"

I stared at her. Out? As in out of here? As in over the fence? As in flight from Stalag Nine (or whatever the number was)?

"Out?" I echoed witlessly, and pressed my hands between my knees in prayer. Please let it be to LA. Oh please!

"Yes, darling. Would you like that? I thought we could have a little shopping outing. You and me."

In LA! LA! LA!

"In Palm Springs."

OK, not LA. But hey! Palm Springs could be a pretty fun place. And it had shops too. Real shops that sold real things, unlike its sister township of Palm Desert where, so far as I remembered, the season's big event was the annual sale of golf wear and medical foundation garments.

"That would be great," I said, and for once the

enthusiasm came completely naturally. Shopping! "I'd really like to get one of those Hawaiian shirts."

Noni turned those sparkling, seriously unbloodshot eyes full on my face.

"Hawaiian shorts?" she said, looking at me as if I'd suddenly painted my face blue and started dancing a jig.

"Shirts," I corrected helpfully.

It didn't help. Her lip curled.

"Well, really darling," – her eyes drifted over me – "I had thought we might find you something a little more suitable to wear. Something more ... ladylike. Something you could wear when Sam comes."

I nearly choked on my granola. Easy to do with all those nut clusters.

"I thought you might like a pretty dress. Or a skirt. A blouse. Something feminine like that."

Now I stared at her with open revulsion. Me? In a dress? I'd rather stick a fork in my eye. I toyed with the idea of doing just that, but I only had the granola spoon and I didn't think the effect would be quite the same.

"Noni," I said, fighting down the urge to scream and tip my cereal over her head. "I don't wear dresses." (Or skirts. Or blouses. Or kitten heels. Or any of that stuff girly-girls tend to go in for.)

She laughed in an irritatingly know-it-all way.

"Well, don't you think, at your age, it's about time you did? Maybe we should get Monsieur Alexander to give you a make-over."

Er ... like, no way!

"Why?" I said trying a) not to sound sulky or b) furious.

She looked at me in that critical way again.

54

"Well, just look at you. You're so pretty and you have such a darling little figure, you should show it off instead of hiding yourself away under all those shapeless ... things."

Right now "those shapeless things" were, to my mind, the height of cool: light but baggy trousers with more pockets than a magician's waistcoat, a cunningly ripped black tank top held together with strategic safety pins and a short-sleeved Celtic print shirt. Noni, Madame Feminine, by contrast, was shoehorned into a close-fitting sundress, matching short-sleeved jacket and a hat the size of a helicopter landing pad. OK, so none of it was shapeless, but they weren't shapes any normal person would have chosen to be seen dead in.

"I don't think so," I said. "I wouldn't feel comfortable. And I like these clothes. A Hawaiian shirt would be cool."

She sighed.

"I suppose you could do with something to wear in this heat," she said.

Not that kind of cool, you moron! I forced myself to smile instead.

"So, can we look at shirts?"

Another sigh.

"Oh, I suppose so," she said, managing to sound both disappointed and disapproving. She didn't give me That Look again, but averted her gaze instead. I ignored the implied insult.

"Hey, thanks, Noni!"

We were going out! Good-bye to Granny's Grotto! First it was Pool God and now this. Things were definitely looking up.

\* \* \*

By the time we reached Palm Springs, Noni seemed to have cheered up, or at least resigned herself to my taste in clothes, and I was starting to feel positively excited. Civilization! (Kind of.) One minute it was all sand and scrub and the next there was a cluster of low, desert-coloured buildings and a handful of palm trees, and then we were cruising down a broad boulevard past shops and nail parlours and banks – only in the kind of buildings no one in England would ever imagine being a bank. It was so great. Everyone was driving those open-top jeeps, even really old people. Excellent!

I saw Esteban glance in the rear-view mirror.

"Where do you want me to take you?" he said.

Noni leaned forward and tapped the back of his seat.

"You can park in the mall," she said. "It's central and there are plenty of stores there. Tell me, can you recommend anywhere for Hawaiian shirts?"

He considered for a moment.

"Rick's Place," he said.

"Is that in the mall?"

And she called herself a movie star. Everyone knew Rick's Place was in Casablanca.

"No, but it's not far. It's on the main drag, just out the far side. Five minutes' walk."

Noni – walk? I thought her type always had to be driven everywhere. I suspected the only reason she condescended to drag herself from one room to another at home was because she couldn't get the car in the house.

I was wrong.

"Fine," she said, brightly. "We can still park in the

mall and walk over."

I gazed out of the window. Mall, huh? That sounded moderately promising. Sadie would have been wetting her pants. Five minutes later I was nearly wetting mine. There were skaters!

As we cruised up alongside a large golden building advertising itself as some kind of Desert Plaza, I caught sight of a group of guys zooming around in an open space at the side, which I assumed had to be a car park. I definitely pressed my nose to the window. I may even have whimpered. All those prisoner sensations came flooding back. Here I was in my gilded cage. There they were – free! I could still see them beyond the wall on the other side of the road, whizzing up and down, leaping and spinning. Soon I would be out of the car and breathing the same air as they were. I clenched my fists and opened them again. At least I wasn't wearing a dress. I might not be able to join them, but I could hold my head up knowing that, if they did notice me, at least they might recognize a kindred soul. Maybe, if they spotted Noni, they would pity me as well. It wouldn't be much, but it would be something.

Esteban pulled in through the automated barrier and found us a covered space in the shade. He came round to open the door and Noni floated out. Neat trick. I propelled myself after her, feeling all elbows and knees, like one of those music stands that always folds the wrong way and gets stuck. Not a neat trick. Not even a trick.

Wow, it was hot. I tried taking a moment to check out the skaters, but Noni was already striding out (how did she do that in those heels?) towards the entrance to the mall, yipping at me to follow. Esteban had grabbed Madge and was holding her under his arm while she yipped too. He saw me looking at the skaters and smiled. He didn't say anything, but tilted his head towards the back of the car, where I saw he'd popped the boot open. I followed him round, curious. What was he planning? Then, as he lifted the lid I saw – my board! I must have given a squeal of excitement, because he made a shushy noise just as Noni turned and, realizing her ewe lamb and current accessory (me) was not trotting obediently in her immediate wake, put one hand on her bony hip and gave The Call.

"Thanks, Esteban," I said. What I really wanted to do was hug him.

The skaters were hard at it in the car park. I gazed at them with open yearning. One of them saw me and waved. I didn't dare wave back, but I flashed him a smile. As we walked into the mall they whizzed across the open concrete and my stomach instantly went into a little knot of longing. The guy who'd waved said "Hi there!" as they passed. I was about to say "Hi!" back when Noni's hand closed on my elbow in that dreaded grip. I was yanked towards the tinted doors, which whispered open to receive us, and was swallowed into the cool marble interior.

We crossed the mall at a brisk trot, past several water features (surprise!) and a large, unattractive sculpture in gold which advertised itself as *The Sun Gives Life to the Desert*, but which looked more like an exploding egg to me. From there we emerged through an impressive set of revolving doors into the sunlight again. Heat! Three minutes in that air-conditioned interior and my body had already forgotten what it was like outside: *The Sun Wallops Katriona Shaw on the Head*. Esteban was pointing out

58

a neat-looking little boutique with – yes! – a picture of Humphrey Bogart airbrushed onto the window and a neato wooden sign saying RICK'S PLACE. Noni lengthened her stride, Esteban sprang ahead to open the door, and we swept in as if we were about to raid the place. (Which I secretly hoped we were.)

Two things happened in quick succession. A huge, muscular man with a shaven head and a moustache that seemed to extend a foot on either side of his face looked up from behind a central counter and, spotting Noni, let out a piercing shriek like a nun caught in the bath. About two nano-seconds later a small white furry object flew out from behind the counter and, spotting Madge, threw itself at her with a similar ear-shredding howl. Instinctively I stepped backwards and reached for the door. If we were under attack, I wanted to be the first to hit the street running. Esteban could take care of Noni. That was what he was paid for.

But it seemed there was only one attack going on, and that was of the doggy variety. The white fluffy thing produced ears and whiskers and a tiny white muzzle lined with even tinier white teeth which it seemed hell bent on sinking into Madge. Meanwhile, the circus strongman look-a-like clapped his hands to his cheeks and squealed, "Oh my God, it's Noni Waters!" then, spotting the mayhem erupting at ankle level, bellowed in an impressive baritone, "Junior!" The Clash of the Small White Furry Things raged my way and I hopped about trying a) not to step on the warring parties and b) not to get in the way of those weeny snapping jaws. Noni flashed a single silent command towards Esteban (impressive, given the sunglasses), then, ignoring the assassination attempt currently in progress against her pride and joy (Madge, not me), zeroed in on the counter and Mr Moustaches, holding out both hands as if she expected him to seize them and cover them in adoring kisses. Even I could see how ridiculous that was as I made a dramatic sideways leap into a rack of highly patterned trousers.

But Noni could obviously read the situation better than I did. As Esteban calmly reached under the trouser rack and straightened up with a writhing ball of white fury snarling in each hand, I saw the moustaches engulf her knuckles and heard the unmistakeable sound of lips going kissy-kissy. OK, so he didn't actually fall on his knees, but it was obvious he was tempted to go for the full carpet dive-and-grovel.

"Miss Waters," he breathed. "I am one of your biggest fans!"

Well, he certainly was big and, judging by the way he was gazing adoringly into her face, yup, definitely a fan. I was impressed. Esteban held up the two dogs, which had stopped trying to kill each other and were now wagging their tails and trying to lick each other's faces.

"Shall I take Madge outside, Miss Noni?" he said.

I couldn't help feeling I was being left out of this little love-fest-cum-psycho-drama.

"I think if you put them down now they can give each other a good sniff and make friends," I said.

It seemed to have worked for Noni and the moustachioed hand-snogger.

Noni gave Esteban an imperious nod. The dogs hit the floor and instantly started to turn circles trying to get a snootful of each other's bums. This done, they then started to chase each other all over the shop, yipping happily. Nobody seemed to mind, so reluctantly I abandoned my role as animal psychiatrist and went back to blending in with the trouser rail.

But Noni wasn't having any of it. She beckoned to me, and Mr M. launched into the whole cheek-slapping, shrieking number again. For someone who looked as if he bent iron bars and hoisted small cars about in his spare time, he was prancing around like a ballet dancer with a wedgie. Which just goes to show.

"A-a-a-h! I don't believe it!" he gasped, like an asthmatic who'd just found his inhaler was empty. I didn't believe it either (whatever it was), but I managed a limp smile.

"It can't be! It has to be! Is this...?" And he began making elaborate gestures in the air around me.

"This is my granddaughter, Katriona."

He placed a large, beautifully manicured paw over his heart.

"Peas in a pod," he breathed. "Peas in a pod!"

I was tempted to retort that when I peed it was *never* anywhere other than the little girls' room, but I merely smiled again and put my hands behind my back in case he fancied going face down into my fingers next.

Esteban, who was watching this exchange with obvious amusement, said, "This is Rick."

Rick held out his hand, but properly this time, and I plucked up enough courage to stick out my own and let him shake it.

"You doll!" he said, but with such a throb in his voice I hadn't the heart to take offence.

Noni clearly felt that I had already taken more than my fair share of the drooling attention on offer and made a brisk chirping sound.

"Katriona would like to look at shirts. Hawaiian shirts," she said, making it sound as if I had taken an unhealthy interest in petty theft and hog-wrestling.

"You do sell Hawaiian shirts?"

Rick swept an arm towards the rear of the shop where Ratdog Madge and Fluffball Junior were tumbling over each other with excitement.

"Do I have shirts!" he said. "Step this way."

And did he ever. They were gorgeous. All of them. Well, nearly all of them. With Rick's advice (I was warming to him rapidly), I ended up with two I simply couldn't choose between: a dove grey number with black Chinese dragons all over it and a blue one with a nifty design of surfers riding huge curling waves. I held them up to Noni to help me decide.

"Lovely, darling," she said, without conviction. She nodded to Rick. "We'll take those two."

Both of them?

"Er ... are you sure?" I said. "I mean, I only really need one. I just can't make my mind up."

Noni looked at me as if I'd sprouted an ear in the middle of my face.

"Then we'll get both," she said, as if addressing a half-witted child, and flung some piece of glittering plastic onto the counter. I'm not sure what it was made of, but I suspect it was to platinum what gold is to mud. She got to sign twice – once on the credit slip and once across some postcard advertising the shop as a favour to Rick, who looked so excited I thought his moustaches were going to fly off.

Esteban retrieved Madge from where Junior appeared to be getting a bit carried away with extending the paw of friendship. Rick snatched up his canine Casanova with a cry of "Not on your first date, you naughty boy!" I took the bag, which had that picture of Humphrey Bogart on the outside and those two amazing shirts on the inside, and followed Noni as she swept to the door. (When you can sweep like Noni, who needs a broomstick?) Esteban played doorman again and, followed by cries of joy and completely unnecessary gratitude, we left.

Whomp! The sun did that surprise heat thing again, but I was so thrilled with the shirts I hardly noticed.

LOCATION: PALM SPRINGS, THE SIDEWALK OUTSIDE RICK'S PLACE
TIME: HIGH NOON

"I need a drink!" Noni announced.

While I wouldn't have objected to something long and cold myself, I didn't really fancy hanging around watching Noni wallop down tankards of gin. Esteban came to my rescue.

"Maybe Katriona would like to look around some more stores. I can go with her while you rest up."

Noni looked as if she were about to shove out an objection, then the obvious merits of the scheme registered and she merely smiled and said, "How very kind of you. Katriona, would you like that?"

Well, yes, Miss Noni, Katriona certainly would.

There was a hotel across the street. We found the lobby bar and settled her at a quiet table with a loud magazine and a large martini. As we were leaving, she called me back and thrust some money at me: "In case you see some other little thing you fancy, darling." It was only when we were outside that I realized it was a fifty dollar bill. That could buy a girl a lot of milk shakes. We headed for the car park and the waiting Jag with its precious cargo. Esteban opened the boot and I reached inside and lifted out my board, running my hands over it lovingly.

63

"OK, young lady," he said. "I'll have to come and watch you, I'm afraid, but I'll keep out of the way. Just don't go breaking any bones or Noni will kill me."

I notice he didn't say "fire me". Maybe she was the kind of employer who took the absolute view of disposing of unwanted staff. Sacking was probably too messy for her. Her husbands were lucky she'd merely settled for divorce.

We walked out of the covered lot and headed for the side of the building. My heart was in my mouth. Maybe the skaters had gone home already, but no, there they were, standing chatting by the corner. I felt suddenly shy, but Esteban gave me a nudge in the back, and as I stepped forward the guy who'd waved spotted me. He dropped his board and skated over.

"Hi there," he said. "I'm Lucas. You want to join us?"

I was in!

They were such cool guys. Really friendly and fun. They were all kind of intrigued by Esteban. One of them asked me if he was my boyfriend, but I just said "No, my probation officer," which made them laugh (in a nervous kind of way). We skated about for a while and then Lucas started to show me a really neat manoeuvre involving a half-spin and a kind of sideways hop. I'd seen it done before, but I'd never tried it myself. He was really patient and it wasn't long before I was beginning to get the hang of it.

"Hey," he said. "You're a fast learner."

"You're a good teacher," I said and we grinned at each other. But I felt guilty about dragging him away from the others.

"I think I need to go practise this," I said. "Thanks."

"No problem. If you need any help, just ask."

I tootled off and tried to concentrate on perfecting the move: skate, spin, hop; skate, spin hop; skate, spin, hop. Hey, it seemed like I'd got it! Feeling bolder, I tried picking up speed: skate, spin, hop; skate, spin hop; skate, spin – oops! The board shot out from under me and I sat down hard. I was vaguely aware of a shout and a yell and the sound of running.

"Are you OK?"

It was Lucas. He held out his hand and I tried to get up with as much dignity as I could muster (which was about zero). I felt like a complete jerk.

"That was amazing!" he said. "You nearly took that guy completely out with your board."

That guy? What guy? Esteban?

"Lucky for him he caught it before it whacked him in the family jewels!"

Everyone laughed. I closed my eyes and groaned.

"I think this is yours," said a voice behind me.

I turned, ready to fall to my knees before Esteban and grovel out my apologies, only the guy standing there holding my board wasn't Esteban.

It was Pool God.

I gulped. I think I may have squeaked.

"Hey," he said. "It's you!"

I wanted to say "No, it isn't!" but I seemed to have temporarily lost the power of speech.

"Neat move," he said. "But you need to use your arms more to keep your balance on the turn."

"Yeah!" said Lucas. "That's what I was telling her."

Men! Anything mildly technical and they immediately assume they can tell you what to do.

Esteban appeared.

"You OK?" he said.

Well, no! I was totally humiliated, not only in front

of the skater guys, but, the ultimate horror, Pool God.
Did it look like I was OK?

"I'm fine," I said, bitterly.

"OK, we need to think about getting back," he said.
He nodded amiably at Pool God.

"Hey there, Taylor. How you doing?"

"Fine. I'm on my way to Rick's. Gotta run."

"See you around," said Esteban.

"You too," said Pool God, but he was smiling at me
when he said it. That smile! Maybe he could forgive
me for nearly making him sing soprano for the rest of
his natural life. I watched him cross the lot and disappear into the mall in a haze of sexiness.

"Come on," said Esteban. "We gotta get back."

"That was cool," said Lucas. "Come skate with us
again sometime."

"I'd like that," I said. "But I don't know if I'll be
able to."

"Prison regulations?" he said.

"Yeah," I said. "Something like that."

This time Esteban brought the car round to the front
of the hotel. No more walking for Noni. Secretly I was
grateful. I didn't want the skater guys spotting me with
her. She looked decidedly unsteady on her pins. And I
didn't think the revolving door was to blame.

LOCATION: PALM DESERT, NONI'S BAR AND
FOUNTAINARIUM
TIME: COCKTAIL HOUR

That evening I put on the dragon shirt and wandered
downstairs to show Noni. She was in the fountainarium propping up the bar and wailing on at Sara
about the fact that Sam Schneider hadn't called. Again.

The way she was going on about it, she made it sound as if somehow it was Sara's fault.

"Are you sure?" she said, stabbing a cocktail stirrer into the ice in her glass as if it was a personal enemy and deserved to die.

Sara was patient.

"Of course I'm sure."

Noni seemed to sag a little.

"He said he would call."

She sounded gloomy now.

"He will. The trouble is, you're just sitting around waiting for the phone to ring."

Noni drew herself up.

"I have not just been sitting around," she said with dignity, then vacuumed up half the contents of the glass, which kind of spoiled the effect.

I hated to intrude upon her in her hour of grief, but she swivelled on the bar stool and spotted me lurking in the doorway.

"There you are!" she said. "I was wondering where you'd disappeared to."

Not true – she'd been wondering where Sam Schneider had disappeared to.

"Is that one of the shirts you bought today? Sara, we got that shirt for Katriona today. Isn't it lovely?"

She had this knack of asking questions she already knew the answer to and then ploughing on before you could reply anyway.

"It's very nice," said Sara.

I saw her eyes flick past me and, looking round, I saw Esteban heading past the pool towards us carrying my skateboard. He slid the glass door open and stuck his head inside.

"Where do you want me to put this?" he asked

mildly, as if he'd just found it a moment before.

Noni narrowed her eyes at him.

"What is it?" she said, with an unnecessarily nasty tone.

"It's my skateboard," I said quickly. "Um..."

"Well, I don't want it in here," Noni began.

Then the phone rang.

Noni sat bolt upright on her stool and shrieked, "Pick it up! Pick it up!" at Sara, which was ridiculous as the phone was just behind her and Sara had to come round the bar to reach it. Then she snapped another look at Esteban and shrieked, "Leave that out there!" He withdrew, closed the door and propped my board against one of the loungers. Fine, I could get it later.

"Hello, Miss Waters's residence."

Noni was already sliding down off the stool and – ye gods! – patting her hair, when Sara put her hand over the receiver and looked at me.

"It's for you," she said.

Noni gave a little moan.

"I'll take it in my room," I said, and ran for the stairs. At least if it was Sadie I could tell her all about my latest humiliating encounter with Pool God. As I left, I saw Noni reach across the bar and help herself to the gin.

LOCATION: PALM DESERT, MY ROOM
TIME: A FEW MINUTES LATER

It wasn't Sadie on the phone. It was my mom.

We had a brief exchange of news. Not much in my case. Even less in hers, if you don't count tiresome descriptions of the preparations for the upcoming conference. But there was one item of interest.

68

"A boy called at the house today asking for you."

"A boy? Who?"

"I'm not sure. I think it was that young man who was at the play. He said his name was Jamie. He left a message for you."

"A message?"

"Yes, you know what a message is, don't you, dear?"

She was being difficult on purpose. Making the most of the boy situation. Maximum parental embarrassment. Rather like the play.

"Just tell me what he said, Mom. Please!"

"Not much, but he left a number. In case you were able to call him anytime."

Oh, wow! Jamie had left me his number! But my mom wasn't done.

"Only make sure you ask Noni before you use the phone."

"She's already said it's OK for me to call people if I want."

My mom gave an audible sniff.

"Yes, well, I would still prefer it if you asked her first."

Was she nuts? The minute I asked Noni if it was OK for me to call a boy in England I'd never hear the last of it. She'd have me strapped to a chair in her private interrogation unit, shining lights in my eyes and sticking pins under my fingernails, before the request had died on my lips.

"OK," I said, crossing my fingers, toes, and anything else I could reasonably manipulate to indicate denial. Of course Mom didn't notice. Oh, the joys of the telephone.

"Now, honey, tell me how you're getting on over there."

She was only trying to ease her conscience and I thought I could at least try and get some of my own back by shoving a feeble complaint her way about what a lousy time I was having. But she wasn't buying it. She even had the nerve to suggest that I was getting the best deal of the summer. Her reasoning: she and Dad were stranded in some industrial gulag in the back of beyond and Einstein was doing time banged up at the local cattery with only a heated blanket and his food dish for company, while I was living in luxury in one of America's most exclusive bits of real estate. To this I pointed out, somewhat coolly, that a) they had chosen to go to Ghastligrad themselves, no one was forcing them into it, and b) at least they had each other to talk to when the going got really tough. As for Einstein, a heated blanket and a dish full of food are all he's ever wanted in life.

We parted on a rather cool note and I went back downstairs to tell Noni that Mom wanted to talk to her. She seemed to have moved beyond speech by now, but she picked up the phone anyway, and within two minutes they had picked a spectacular fight with each other. Typical. I'd heard it so many times before, I decided to leave them to it. I trudged back up to my room, where I flopped down on the bed, only now I didn't feel sleepy. I should have brought more books with me – I'd already finished the one I'd begun on the flight – but then I noticed some books of Noni's on one of the cabinets.

I hopped off the bed and went over to cast a jaundiced eye over them. It turned out to be a surprisingly interesting collection: a couple of airport novels, a well-thumbed copy of *Anna Karenina* and a small volume I didn't recognize. I took it out and looked at it. *Acting*

*Against Character*, it was called, by someone with the improbable name of Sándor Keczkes. One of Noni's acting manuals, I guessed. Huh! So it wasn't all cheekbones and instinct. Maybe once upon a time she had actually put some hard work into those acting skills. Maybe I could learn something myself? Sándor Keczkes. Now just how did you pronounce that? I was more or less OK with the "Sándor" and pretty good for the "K" and the "e", but then the whole thing seemed to get hit by shrapnel and limp off to sit out the second half with its leg in the air. I dare say I wouldn't ever find out. Not that it mattered, anyway. The book was dated 1968. Sándor K. was probably already pushing up the daisies by now. Maybe I should ask Mr Jeffries, my drama teacher, when I was back at school. I flipped it open and settled myself back on the bed with a yawn.

LOCATION: PALM DESERT
TIME: SOMETIME IN THE WEE SMALL HOURS

I must have dropped off to sleep because when I heard the crash, for a moment I thought I was back home in Oxford and couldn't understand a) why Einstein wasn't asleep on my feet and b) why the door wasn't where it ought to be. I floundered around and tried to get my ears to work. Nothing. Then outside, somewhere below my window, I heard a long, low moan and a whimper and then a series of staccato barks that rose rapidly to a hysterical falsetto, made themselves comfortable there and settled into a rhythmic shrieking. By then I was already off the bed and sprinting for the stairs. Seconds later I was in the fountainarium with my face pressed against the glass.

Noni was lying sprawled beside the pool at an

71

awkward angle, Madge running in frantic circles beside her. I yanked open the door and ran over.

"Noni!" I said. "Are you all right?"

More moaning. I think she said something like "I'm dying", but it could have been "crying" or "trying" or even "flying". She rolled her head about and opened her eyes a fraction. I felt rather than saw the exposed slits focus on me, then close again.

"It's all your fault," she said, quite distinctly, and went back to moaning.

What?

At least she could still speak, even if it was gibberish.

"Stay there," I said. "Don't move." (Apart from twitching and groaning, that is.) "I'll go get Esteban."

Easier said than done. Where was I going to find him, or anyone, at this time of night? I had a feeling he and Sara lived somewhere on the property, but where? I didn't want to waste time stumbling through the bushes in the dark. Then I remembered the phone. I went into the house and looked at the one on the bar. It was the same as the one in my room. Good. There were several buttons: one marked "Sara", one marked "Esteban" and one which said "Est/Sara". I tried this one first. Bingo! Sara answered on the third ring.

"Hello?"

"Sara, it's Kat. I need your help. Noni's out by the pool. She's fallen and I think she's hurt herself."

Sara was brisk. She didn't sound alarmed. Or surprised.

"She has? OK. You wait there with her, honey. We're coming right now."

I went out and told Noni they were on their way. No response.

A few minutes later they appeared round the side of

the house. I hurried over to meet them.

"Is she conscious?" was Sara's first question.

"Kind of," I said. "She opened her eyes a bit and spoke to me."

"That's good. What did she say?"

Um. Tricky one that.

"I'm not sure," I lied. "Madge was barking in my ear."

Esteban was already ahead of us on his knees beside Noni, holding her hand. As we caught up with him he looked up at Sara.

"Call an ambulance," he said. "I think she may have broken her ankle."

"No-o-o!" (This came from Noni, not Sara.) "Help me upstairs."

Esteban looked back down at her.

"I'm not going to try and move you," he said. "You need medical attention."

"I'm fine! Really!"

Her voice was getting stronger now.

"I'll go call 911," said Sara, and went into the house. Noni started to cry.

"Can you get the dog?" said Esteban. "She's kind of in the way."

Kind of? Madge was still running in ever-decreasing circles, yapping like a thing possessed. I bent down and picked her up. She wriggled and squealed. I stroked her head hard, pulling at her weeny little ears, and said, "Shush!" She shushed. Then she licked my hand and looked up at me. The little madam. I could have sworn she was enjoying the whole thing. Some types thrive on excitement. Madge clearly lived for disaster.

"Can you tell me what happened?" Esteban was saying to Noni. I stepped back to give them a little space and then I noticed something in the pool. I walked over to the side and looked down into the eerie blue-green water. There was a dark shape lying on the bottom, clear and unmistakeable in the stillness.

It was my skateboard.

"Er, Esteban," I said. "I need to show you something."

He got up and came over. He looked into the pool. He looked at the skateboard. He looked at me. Madge lifted her head and licked my chin and gave what sounded unpleasantly like a doggy-type chuckle.

"Oh boy," said Esteban. Which just about summed it up.

We both went back and looked down at Noni. She must have sensed she'd been rumbled, because she'd closed her eyes again and didn't look like she was interested in opening them in a hurry.

I put my hands on my hips like some soap opera queen (well, the hand that wasn't clutching Madge, that is) and frowned.

"Were you trying out my skateboard?" I said.

She did the head rolling thing again, eyes wide shut.

"I said it was your fault," she muttered.

Nice try.

"My fault?"

More twitching.

"You shouldn't have left it out there."

"You told Esteban to leave it outside."

Mumble mumble. Something like "He should have known I didn't mean it." It was probably the same line she used when it came to discussing how much she might have promised to pay her soon-to-be-ex-husbands when the divorce came through. Esteban was busy propping her left foot up on a cushion from one of the loungers. Noni squealed and clutched at his arm.

Sara reappeared. She was carrying a blanket, which he took from her and laid over Noni just as gently as I'd seen him do the other night.

"The ambulance is on its way," she said.

Noni began to cry in earnest.

"I can't let anyone see me like this," she pleaded. "No one must know. Kat! Tell him I don't want anyone to know. He must understand."

Why was she appealing to me all of a sudden? Understand what? OK, the mascara was looking a little runny, but maybe we could arrange to pick up Monsieur Alexander on the way to the hospital. I went back and sat down next to her. Madge seemed to have calmed down enough for me to let her go, and she trotted straight over and began to lick Noni's face. Noni flapped her away.

"You have to get that ankle looked at," I said. "Even I can see it's already really swollen. Sara's gone for some ice."

"No, no," she said. "I'll be fine."

"You need to get it X-rayed," I reasoned. "It doesn't hurt, you know. I've had it done loads of times."

Which was true – Katriona Shaw, the most accident-prone kid in the entire Oxford area. They already knew me so well in the casualty department at the John Radcliffe that each time the car carrying me from my latest disaster drew up outside, all the nurses gathered in the doorway waving and calling to me by name.

"I know that!" She sounded irritated.

Well, excuse me! I was only trying to help. One thing I wasn't about to mention was the fact that I suspected and she must have known (along with Esteban and

75

Sara) that she was drunk as a skunk. Not something you can keep from your average doctor. They're trained to spot that kind of thing. OK, so maybe it was the embarrassment factor she was worried about. Tough. Grandpa Zack had an expression for facing unpleasant situations, especially ones of your own making: "Suck it up!" he would say. "You just gotta suck it right up." Except in Noni's case the problem was that she had been sucking it up like an ant-eater finally coming off a calorie-controlled, no-ant diet and faced with a termite mound marked "Insert tongue here."

Noni looked around wildly, then gestured for me to come closer. Obediently, I leaned over her. Mistake. She may have broken her ankle, but she still had a grip like a vice. I felt my wrist crunching in her fingers. Maybe the X-ray department would find they were getting two for the price of one.

"If Sam gets to hear about this, he may change his mind about the picture," she whispered in my ear. Make that "whispered desperately in my ear". It took me a moment to figure out what she meant.

"You mean Mr Schneider?" I whispered back, only without the desperation.

She nodded dumbly. Her grip tightened on my wrist. Yow! At least I still had one hand free. I could probably get in one good punch before I blacked out. Explain that to the medics, Noni.

"OK," I said. "I understand."

I looked at Esteban.

"Do you know where they'll be taking her?"

"Either the main public hospital, or we could get them to go to the clinic. The clinic's much smaller, quieter. Kind of exclusive. It's where the local celebrities usually go for minor ops and stuff when they want to keep it private."

I guess that meant all those cosmetic tweakings.

"Do they do broken ankles?"

He shrugged.

"The way they charge, I'm sure they can do whatever's necessary."

"Can you get them to take her there? I mean, it's not like she's having a heart attack or a stroke or anything like that, is it?"

"I heard that!" Noni said behind me.

We ignored her.

Sara opened the door and called out that the ambulance was at the gate.

"I'll go talk to them," said Esteban.

LOCATION: A VERY EXPENSIVE CLINIC, SOMEWHERE IN THE DESERT
TIME: THE EVEN TINIER WEE SMALL HOURS

The clinic was everything Esteban had promised and more. From the soft swish of the automatic doors to the soft swish of the automatic receptionists, it breathed exclusivity and expense.

I hated it on sight.

Give me the good old John Radcliffe: NHS on a Saturday with the kids with peas up their noses and pans stuck on their heads and the awful roaring drunks. Let's face it, life is a war zone where we have to put aside our differences and pull together in the face of a common enemy: human stupidity. And how much more stupid does it get than a sixty-two-year-old woman drinking way too many martinis, trying out her fifteen-year-old granddaughter's skateboard, and breaking her ankle in the process? Put Noni in Casualty in the UK and the staff would be gathered round her bed of pain to have a good laugh at her expense, and well-deserved too. Here, you would have thought minor royalty had paid them the honour of a surprise visit.

The first procedure she was subject to appeared to be a swift yet thorough examination of her credit card, the result of which must have been positive, as white-coated men and women of a distinctly medical flavour suddenly oozed out of every cranny and began to go through a ritual alarmingly similar to the one I'd seen performed by Rick, the moustachioed shirt vendor, only hours earlier. Which was probably all very healing for her bruised ego, but didn't appear to be doing a whole lot for her on the ankle front.

I began to get annoyed. It was half past one in the morning. I was tired. Esteban was tired. And Noni, the prime source of all our grief and woe, who, to my mind, should have been strapped to a metal gurney that first saw service during World War II and given a grilling about her alcohol intake by some over quali-fied, overworked, underpaid no-nonsense medic from the Indian subcontinent, was instead being wafted through scented corridors by a young doctor who was a dead ringer for Barbie's Ken, and having her hand patted by a young woman who obviously modelled for *Vogue* as her day job and only worked in the clinic at night as a form of service to the community.

"Excuse me," I said. "Will this take long?"

Ken turned and noticed me at last. Maybe I should have rustled Noni's fifty dollars earlier. Maybe that would have got me some attention.

"I don't want to bother you," I said. "But my grandmother is kind of eager to get herself patched up and back home as quickly as possible so she can rest up and get herself better."

Note: for "rest up" read "sleep it off".

"And she doesn't really want anyone else to know what happened."

The doctor nodded and gave an expensive kind of half-smile. Yikes! Was that going on the bill?

"I understand," he said. "I do assure you this clinic insists on absolute discretion."

What? "Absolute discretion"? Wasn't that some kind of cocktail?

Esteban appeared at my side. He took hold of my elbow – gently, you see, it can be done – and said, "Miss Shaw is simply concerned about her grandmother."

The doctor transferred his gaze from me to him and treated us to a smile so dazzling I took half a pace backwards.

"Why don't you take a seat in our lounge?" he said. "Someone will bring you a coffee or a cold drink while you wait."

Well, why not indeed? There didn't seem a whole lot else to do there except tiptoe the carpeted halls wondering how much of the artwork was original and flip through back issues of *The Cosmetic Surgeons' Monthly*.

We hit the lounge. Esteban asked for a coffee. I did the same, which raised an eyebrow and an enquiry as to whether we wanted decaf. We both said "No".

I finished my coffee and yawned. Esteban looked at me.

"I guess that was decaf," he said.

"I guess it was," I said, and promptly fell asleep on his shoulder.

Well, it wasn't like Noni was dying in there.

\* \* \*

She hadn't broken anything. There were mutterings about torn ligaments and other medical jargon. The word "sprain" seemed popular. The upshot was that she was to rest her leg and not put any weight on it for at least two weeks. Doctor Ken handed over a bottle of painkillers and carefully looked at a distant point somewhere beyond my left shoulder while he suggested that it wasn't a good idea to mix them with alcohol. Ahem. Point duly noted.

We wheeled Noni out to the car while she sank as low in the chair as she could in case there were photographers lurking in the bushes. But there were no tell-tale flashes from the undergrowth and we got her in and away undetected. Back at the house Esteban simply scooped her out of the back of the car and carried her in and up the stairs in his arms, like Scarlett O'Hara, while I trundled pointlessly behind with the wheelchair like an extra from *E.R.* No, on second thoughts, make that *E.T.* Sara followed with a pair of crutches. I wished I'd opted for those. Then at least I could have pretended to be a real character, a character with a name. Even it was Long John Silver.

Esteban and Sara settled her into bed as comfortably as possible. Sara put the crutches away in a cupboard on the opposite side of the room from the bed. A wise precaution. We reckoned she'd probably sobered up enough to have a painkiller, which she took without too much fuss. Her main concern still seemed to be what Sam Schneider would do when he found out what had happened. We told her there was no point losing sleep over it now (2.20 a.m.) and she treated us to a baleful glare. Sara said she would sit up with her, which I thought was pretty noble. We closed the door on a stream of petulant twittering and I followed Esteban downstairs to say "good night". He pulled at the brim of his hat and grinned at me.

"You go get yourself some sleep," he said. "You don't need to worry about your grandmother. She's in good hands and, well, she ain't exactly going anywhere in a hurry, now."

I could see the wisdom of this.

"I will," I said. "And … well … thanks for everything today." And I didn't just mean the emergency dash through the night with Noni, the sprain victim.

He reached out and touched me on the arm.

"No problemo, princess," he said and stepped out into the warm darkness.

Back upstairs I popped my head round Noni's door. The petulant twittering had died away into the steady rasp-whistle-rasp of Noni at rest. Sara had stretched out on the couch and she gave me a little wave. I waved back. Madge plopped off the end of the bed and ran over to me.

"What do you want?" I whispered.

Sara made shooing gestures with her hands, indicating I should take her with me, which was probably a good idea in case she disturbed Noni.

"OK," I said, picking her up. "But if you snore, you're out."

She did her wriggly, face-licky thing.

"And you can cut that out as well."

But secretly, I was kind of pleased to have her. I mouthed "good night" to Sara and tottered off in search of some serious shut-eye of my own.

I don't know what they put in the painkillers, but Noni was still asleep when I woke up at around a quarter to ten. I was glad to find Sara had abandoned her all-night vigil and was now sitting in the kitchen drinking a well-earned cup of coffee. Frankly, if she'd been sipping champagne from a jewel-encrusted goblet, it would still have been well-earned. She fixed me a world-class omelette with what smelled suspiciously like fresh-baked rolls. I had reached the final plate-licking, finger-sucking stage when the phone rang: an internal call. Noni was awake and demanding attention. (With Noni the two usually did go hand in hand.) Sara duly snapped into room service mode and trotted off to attend to her needs while I found the dishwasher and loaded my dirty dishes. I was heading back up to my room when the intercom by the door buzzed like an angry wasp. Sara came clattering down the stairs and answered.

"Oh God," she said. "It's Monsieur Alexander. I'd forgotten he was coming this morning." She spoke into the phone and pressed some button which presumably released the gates at the entrance to the driveway. "Would you be a sweetie and let him in while I go and see what Noni wants me to do about him?"

I noticed there was none of that "Miss Noni" nonsense this morning. Maybe Sara had had a rougher night than I thought. I waited by the door until I heard the crunch of tyres passing and then, shortly after, approaching footsteps and a ring at the door. What now? I was still awaiting further instructions like "raise the drawbridge" or "scream 'Go away! Go away!'"

Nothing. Good. I was kind of curious to find out what the fabled Monsieur Alexander was like. I opened the door expecting – I don't exactly know what – a Hercule Poirot look-alike? California's answer to Graham Norton? Some exotic Gallic gnome with a line in loud shirts, lace cravats and velvet trousers?

OK, so I was close with the loud shirt. It was the Ginger Giant. He was sporting the familiar Hawaiian look, only a different model this time: no surfers and hibiscus; instead, a subtle motif of red radios emitting streams of black music against a blue background.

"Heck," he said in that joke accent he'd tried on to such good effect before. "I weren't expecting to find you answering t'door."

Well, there was news. I thought the surprise was all mine. He ambled past me into the hallway.

"What's the matter? Sara gone on strike? Not that I'd blame her if she had."

There wasn't any way I could have stopped him even if I'd wanted to. I could always have run screaming after him and head-butted him in the back, but he was so huge he probably wouldn't even have noticed. OK, so he was big, but not deaf. I was about to suggest he wait while I went to find Sara when she appeared again and called down that it was OK to come on up. She didn't look too happy. Ginger Giant spotted it at once.

"Now what's up?" he said a tone that suggested that a regular feature of visits to Château Noni involved something or other being "up". He seemed to expect me to follow him, so I did. I didn't like to mention that whatever else might be up, I could guarantee it wasn't our resident invalid, but I figured he'd find that out soon enough. Besides, I was still trying to wrap my head around Ginger Giant as Monsieur Alexander. The

"Alexander" worked for me. But "Monsieur"? With that accent? I mean, puh-leez!

We crossed the landing and entered Noni's room. I had half-expected "Monsieur" Alexander's shoulders to stick in the door-frame, but he made it on through. (Noni had probably had extra-wide doors fitted especially for him.) She was sitting propped up on pillows trying to look both brave and tragic and doing a pretty good job of it. When she saw us (or at least, when she saw Mr Beautification) she held out both hands, tipped her head back (she even had pretty nostrils, can you believe?) and cried in a ringing voice: "Alexander! Thank God! You have to help me!"

Alexander appeared unimpressed by this Academy Award winning performance. But then, maybe she carried on like that every time he came round. He slung his case onto a chair and went over to the end of the bed.

"All right," he said. "What've you done now? From where I'm standing you don't look too bad."

Noni produced a handkerchief from somewhere in the depths of her gauzy sleeve and applied it to the corner of her eye.

"I've had the most terrible night, Alexander. Dreadful! Sara, you tell him what happened; I don't think I can bear to talk about it."

Good. I didn't think I could bear to listen. Alexander looked at Sara. Sara looked at the ceiling and sighed.

"Well..." she began.

Noni flopped back tragically against the pillows as if the mere prospect of listening to the tale of her "ordeal" had exhausted her. Suddenly I felt really annoyed. The whole thing was ridiculous. She'd had the three of us leaping around after her all night because of a stupid accident that was her own silly fault, and now she was trying to make out she deserved all the sympathy. Time for some plain speaking.

"I'll tell you what happened," I said crossly. "She had a few too many last night, found my skateboard, fell off and sprained her ankle. That's all."

"Katriona!"

Her shriek would have put an express train to shame. The speed and force with which she hurled the pillow at my head would have impressed the Olympic selectors. If her aim hadn't let her down, that is. Alexander caught the pillow and laughed.

"Is that true?" he said.

"No!" yelled Noni.

"Yes," Sara and I said together.

"Two against one," said Alexander. "Anyway, I don't care what you've done as long as you haven't damaged your face. And you can stop scowling like that as soon as you like. You'll get lines."

Like the dawn rising, the scowl lifted – or rather the scowl lines vanished, but the scowl somehow managed to linger on. Maybe it was in her hair. Or her ears. Scowly ears. Scary!

He walked round the bed and looked at her. Closely. She glared back.

"So," he said, at last. "What am I to do with you, then? How's the timetable looking regarding Sam..."

Noni clamped her hands over her ears (and I don't think it was to hide the scowl).

"Don't say it!" she wailed. "Don't even mention it! You mustn't breathe a word of this to anyone. No one must know. If *he* gets to hear..."

Her voice trailed away, suggesting boundless horror.

"He doesn't have to know you'd been drinking,"

Alexander said, reasonably enough.

Noni shot him a poisonous glance.

"I didn't mean that," she snapped in a startling departure from wounded heroine mode. "He mustn't hear anything at all. If he finds out I can't walk, that will be it. He'll look for someone else. I know him, the rat. Probably some talentless hag like Jeanette Fleurie."

Wow. I knew the movie was supposed to be about the "sexual power of the older woman", but, frankly, the kind of performance Noni was pulling off now, they could have dumped Arnie, cast her in *Terminator 4* and watched the cream of Hollywood ripped to shreds. Action movies? Who needs them! Noni could build up a body count of genocidal proportions strapped in an iron lung.

"Well, I don't think you need worry," said Sara. "None of us is going to say anything to anyone. You know that. And you've been waiting for Mr Schneider to call for weeks. By the time he does get round to it, I expect you'll be back on your feet and..."

The phone rang by the bed.

Sara stopped speaking (forgetting to close her mouth in the process) and looked at it as if it had suddenly grown fangs and a tail. So did Noni. I can't speak for Monsieur Alexander because I was behind him, but I can speak for me and I positively goggled at it. There was a moment's silence. It rang again.

"Well," said Alexander. "Aren't you going to answer it, then?"

Sara reached out and picked it up as if she thought it might electrocute her.

"Hello, Miss Waters's residence."

Squawking noises. Sara's eyebrows shot up. Noni mouthed "Who is it?" like some demented mime artist and clutched for the phone.

"Just one moment." Sara clapped her hand over the receiver and stared at us with something that looked horribly like panic and despair. More mouthing and clutching from Noni. Sara brushed her aside with the air of someone who knows disaster looms and can't be bothered with the niceties any more.

"It's Sam Schneider," she said. "He wants to talk to Noni."

Noni threw us all out while she spoke to him.

We trooped downstairs and stood in the hallway, looking at each other, not knowing quite what to say. Then Sara offered to make coffee and we retired to the kitchen for a council of war.

"What's she going to say to him if he wants to see her any time soon?" I knew it was the question in all our minds, but I had to ask anyway.

Sara hit the button on the espresso maker and shrugged.

"I don't want to think about it," she said.

"She'll find some way to put him off," Monsieur Alexander said, with more confidence than I suspected he actually felt. "She's nobody's fool, our Noni."

Hello! He was talking about a sixty-two-year-old woman who had got drunk and nearly broken her ankle falling off a skateboard.

Esteban walked in.

"Hey, there," he said. He and Monsieur Alexander did some complicated handshake thing which finished with them punching each other on the arm. Guys. I guess they don't change much with age. Apart from growing hair in places we really wish they wouldn't. I could see a tangle of tight ginger curls fighting for supremacy in the open neck of Monsieur Alexander's shirt. Oh, yuk! Don't think about the body hair. Do *not* think about the body hair!

Sara said something to Esteban in Spanish, about Noni, I guessed, given the way he immediately looked up at the ceiling in the general direction of Noni's room and shook his head.

We drank our coffee in silence. The suspense was horrible.

At last a light flashed and went out on the display unit on the telephone on the countertop.

"She's off the phone," said Sara. "What should we do? I'm not going back up there alone."

"We'll all go," I said. "Safety in numbers. Besides, you've put the crutches out of reach so she can't exactly leap from her bed of pain and stab us all to death with her earrings. And, come on, we're all dying to know what she said."

"If she'll tell us," said Sara.

Monsieur Alexander's eyes narrowed.

"She'll tell us," he said. "In less than half an hour her face will be completely at my mercy. She'll tell."

I looked at him with new admiration.

In the end none of this was necessary. She sang like a bird. A strange, mad, delusional bird, but she sang.

She was sitting up in bed with a smile on her face and a new light in her eyes. OK, so the smile was a bit rigid round the edges and the light was more of a manic gleam than a sparkle, but she always looked like that. We trooped in and tried to look mildly interested rather than desperately curious.

"Well," rumbled Monsieur Alexander. (I really was going to have to find another name for him.)

"He wants me to make the picture!" she blurted out and gave a high, girlish laugh. Make that a high, hysterical laugh.

"He does? That's so great! I'm so pleased for you!"

This was Sara, who then displayed her own line in madness by rushing over to the bed and kissing Noni on the cheek. I could see she meant it too. It was rather sweet. It was also a tribute to Noni that she could inspire that kind of affection in her employees. If only she could have inspired it in her family.

Noni simpered, then rolled her eyes, rather like Madge.

"He's coming here to talk it through with me!"

Her merry tone was becoming a little forced now.

"He is?" Sara sounded surprised. "When?"

"Three days from now."

"What?" This was me.

"You told him about your ankle, then, and he didn't mind?" Sara asked.

Noni rolled her eyes so wildly I thought they were about to disappear into her head.

"No!"

This came out as a strangled croak.

"'No' as in he didn't mind?"

Noni gurgled a moment and clutched at the covers.

"You didn't tell him, did you?" No beating about the bush for Monsieur Alexander.

"No!"

She barely whispered the word and crammed her fingers into her mouth.

There was a moment's silence. "Stunned silence" is the expression, I believe.

"OK," I said when it had begun to get really painful. "Let's get this straight. Sam Schneider called and asked to meet you here in three days' time, and you said 'yes'."

Noni nodded. Basic acting exercise number one.

"But nothing about the ankle."

Noni shook her head. Basic acting exercise number two.

She took her fingers out of her mouth long enough to say "Help!" in a tiny voice, and then she put them back.

Help? She was beyond help.

"You'll just have to call him back and rearrange."

Out came the fingers again. Good. It was getting nasty in there.

"I can't," Noni said, then, in a slightly stronger voice. "I daren't."

"I could call him," I offered, in a spirit of helpfulness I didn't really feel.

"Don't you dare do any such thing, Missy!"

Nothing wrong with the volume now.

"Well, what are we supposed to do? What are you going to do?"

Noni tilted her chin and tried to look resolute.

"I'll just have to learn to walk again," she said, like the plucky, wheelchair-ridden heroine of some awful tear-jerker.

"No way, Tiny Tim," said Monsieur Alexander. "If what they tell me is right, you can't even stand up now, let alone put enough weight on your ankle to walk."

"I can try!"

"No, you can't." Esteban putting in his money's worth.

Noni began to pluck at the sheets and wail. Madge, who had been lying on the bed next to her, sat up and looked at her with interest. No apparent sympathy, just interest.

"We have to think of something!"

Oh great, it was "we" now, was it? Typical. Noni creates huge mess, everyone else has to figure out ways to clear it up.

"We could take the strapping off just while he's here, and you could stay sitting down the whole time."

We considered this for a moment, then Esteban shook his head.

"It's too risky," he said.

I had to agree.

"I agree," I said. (You see, I just had to.) "What if something happens so she has to get up? It'll look too weird if she doesn't. It's one thing for this guy to suspect she's hurt her leg. It's another for him to end up thinking she's paraplegic."

Noni emitted a muffled howl. Madge wagged her tail.

Now it was Monsieur Alexander's turn with the bright ideas.

"I could be giving you a pedicure," he said. "Nobody would expect you to be walking around then."

I liked this one; I thought this one had potential. But Noni wasn't having any of it.

"I am not meeting with Sam Schneider while you fiddle about with my feet," she said. "How long does the average pedicure last? What if he stays all day?"

The ideas had temporarily run dry. We all stood and looked at each other, frowning with the effort of trying to think of new and ever more unlikely schemes.

"I give up," said Monsieur Alexander.

"Beats me for now," said Esteban.

Sara merely shrugged.

I shook my head.

"What you need is a double," I said, just to demonstrate how impossible the whole thing was.

There was moment's stillness, as if everyone had been frozen in time, then they all looked at me.

Meaningfully.

"What?" I said. "OK, it's a stupid idea, but it's no worse than any of yours."

"It's not stupid," said Monsieur Alexander. "It's downright bloody brilliant. Why didn't we think of it? It's so obvious. And it was staring us in the face the whole time."

I stared him in the face.

"Oh really?" I said. "And where are we going to find someone who looks like Noni in the next three days?"

Monsieur Alexander smiled a wolfish smile. Sara gave a squeak. Esteban looked at me then looked away, apparently embarrassed.

"Oh no!" I said. "No! No!"

I began to back towards the door.

"Yes!" shrilled Noni. "Yes!"

Monsieur Alexander reached out one huge paw and seized me by the chin. I glared up at him.

"Peas in a pod," he said.

Now where had I heard that before?

"No!" I squealed again, as best I could with my jaw in a vice. "I don't look anything like her. I'm fifteen. FIFTEEN, for crying out loud!"

And believe me, was I crying out loud. As if my life depended on it.

"You're all as mad as she is!" I shouted. "I can't do it, and I won't!"

I jerked my head out of Monsieur Alexander's bear-like grip and ran out of the room.

"Katriona-a-a-a!"

Noni's voice followed me along the landing like a siren. And I don't mean the kind that sits on a rock combing her hair.

The siren wail was followed by a mighty, rushing wind: Monsieur Alexander. I put on a spurt and virtually threw myself into my room, hurling the door shut behind me. Fast, but not fast enough. Where there should have been the satisfying ker-lick of the catch in the lock, there was a dull ker-thud as the door bounced off Man Mountain. He caught it by the handle and stood there, smiling gently.

"Go away," I yelled.

The smile never wavered.

"Do you mind if I come in?" he said.

"I won't do it!" I shouted. "It's crazy. You're all crazy."

"That's probably true," he said, in a mild voice. "May I come in anyway?"

I shrugged and went and sat on the end of the bed. Ben Nevis (now there was a good name for him) ambled in and leaned against the door-frame. It creaked, but held.

"Noni really needs your help," he said.

"Fine," I said. "She can have it. Within reason. What she can't expect is my body and soul."

With the emphasis on "body". I doubted Noni would know what to do with a soul.

He looked at me, still calm, as if weighing me up.

"It won't work," I said. "For two reasons. One: there's no way I could pass as Noni. I don't look anything like her. I don't act like her. And two: even if I did, I wouldn't do it."

"Why not?"

"Why not?" What a stupid question. "Because ... because ... I ... it's ... because it's nuts. That's why."

He shrugged. The foundations of the house shifted slightly.

"Noni is desperate to have this part," he said.

"Noni is desperate, period," I said.

"She needs to do this."

"I don't care."

"Why not? I do."

That was a poser.

"OK, put it this way: I hope she gets to do the movie. But she got herself into this situation. I didn't. You didn't. It's not my problem."

Mental note: Noni is, and always has been, everybody's problem.

He just stood there looking at me, thinking God knows what to himself. Now I was the one feeling desperate.

"I can't do it."

I didn't mean to sound so pathetic.

"Nobody can make me do it."

Firmer, angrier – that was better.

"No," he said. "They can't. And they won't. So, let's go back in there, you and me, and talk it through with Noni."

"No!"

"No? So what are you going to do? Lock yourself in here for the rest of your stay? I don't think so. Now, how sure are you that you don't look like her?"

I resisted the urge to run into the bathroom and check the mirror.

"I have no boobs, for starters."

I can't believe I actually said that. I thought for a moment he was going to smile. His jaw twitched, but then he appeared merely to be grinding his teeth.

"OK. So why don't we tell her that you've agreed to let me make you over to look like her and then, when she sees you don't, she'll have to drop it?"

Hmmm. It seemed like a reasonable idea. So why did I smell a rat?

"Umm..." I said.

He spread his hands.

"And even if you do, you still don't have to agree to anything else."

This was true.

"That way she can't blame you for not trying to help."

Also true. Horribly true. If Noni thought I could have helped her out of this mess but that I'd refused to do it, my life wouldn't be worth living. Almost as not worth living as if I let them dress me up as her and release me on an unsuspecting Sam Schneider. Ah yes, Sam Schneider. The final frontier. What were the chances of a shrewd guy like him, a guy who'd known Noni for years, being fooled by me? About one in a gazillion. Putting it like that, I felt better. The whole scheme was obviously doomed before it got off the ground.

"OK," I said. "I'll do that. But no more."

"Fine. Come on, then. Let's go and talk it over with Noni before she bursts a blood vessel in there."

As we walked back along the landing, I remembered another one of Grandpa Zack's favourite phrases. I could almost hear him whispering it in my ear: "Softly, softly, catchee monkey." I snuck a suspicious look at

Monsieur Alexander. His broad, freckled face looked comfortable and kindly. Never mind monkeys, I could still smell that rat. And it wasn't the otherwise fragrant Madge.

When we announced I was up for the big transformation (yeah, right) the reactions varied. Esteban looked like the steering wheel of the Jag had burst into flames in his hands; Sara looked as if she'd swallowed a pickled lobster whole; and Noni burst into tears amid cries of "Darling, you'll do this for me?" Anyone would have thought I'd offered to donate a kidney. Looking back, that would have been the less traumatic option.

Followed by cries from Noni of "Use anything you need!" Monsieur Alexander wheeled me into another room I never even knew existed: Noni's private dressing room/sitting room/beauty parlour, etc. It was huge and it was gorgeous, with an uninterrupted curve of windows offering a view far out over the desert. I wondered why I'd never been allowed in here before.

Sara brought in Mr Beauty's bag of tricks while I (currently cast as the Beast) was scooted into the bathroom. Monsieur Alexander stood behind me as I stared glumly at my reflection, and tugged at my hair.

"A couple of inches should do it," he said, pulling it out sideways from my head and letting it slip through his fingers.

"What?!"

"I'll need to take off a couple of inches."

"Hang on a minute! You're not cutting my hair."

I felt him sigh behind me. The soap rattled in its scallop-shaped dish.

"Look, either we're doing this properly or we might as well not bother."

I scowled. Not bothering suited me just fine.

"I think it would look nice," Sara offered from the doorway.

Nice try, Sara.

"Two inches. How long will that take to grow back? Come on. And you need tidying up. You've some shocking split ends here. Do us all a favour."

Five minutes later he had me head-down in the sink and was massaging some noxious gunk into my scalp. Great, all my life I'd wanted to smell like a grapefruit with back notes of skunk. The citrus-dog combo was followed by something more acceptable, if a bit on the floral side, and next thing I was swathed in towels and being frogmarched (how do you march frogs anyway – don't they kind of leap about from side to side?) over to an alarmingly business-like chair by the window. Last time I was in a chair like that, a dentist was doing something unpleasant to my back teeth and I was dribbling out of the side of my mouth and trying not to kick the nurse on the shins. I could feel my tongue shrivelling in my mouth and sweat breaking out on my palms. As if sensing my discomfort, Sara asked if I would like something to drink. Did I ever! OK, so it was only 11 a.m., but my first thought was "whatever Noni was on last night, and plenty of it". Given there was no friendly anaesthetist on hand, any other non-medical aids to oblivion seemed the only way forward. I opted for a glass of water.

"You did say just two inches, didn't you?" I said, after Sara had gone.

He hit me on the top of my (towelled) head with a comb. Cheek! I bet he never did that to Noni.

"Did I?"

I didn't like the sound of that, but I didn't know

what else to say? "Don't"? "Help"? What would Noni say?

"Ruin my hair and I'll sue you," I said.

A rumble of amusement from behind.

"Very funny."

I heard the ominous clack-clack of the scissors and pressed my eyes closed. Then he was on me like a power-strimmer on an overgrown hedge.

It was all over mercifully quickly. Then came the finger drying. What was wrong with a quick blast with the old Morphy Richards, I wanted to know. Too drying was the answer, amid a flurry of fluffing and tugging. (Wasn't that the point?) But for someone whose hands looked like catchers' mitts and whose fingers wouldn't have been out of place in a pork butcher's sausage display, he was surprisingly gentle. I was just starting to get into the whole rhythm of it when he stopped (typical) and spun the chair round to look at me. Minor snippety adjustments, then a sudden dart and spear with a long-handled comb. Hair tumbled over my eyes.

"Your natural parting falls there, to the left," he said. "Not down the middle."

"I've always parted it down the middle," I said, wounded.

"Not a good reason," he said, patiently. "I'm trying to make you look like a movie star here, not Ozzie Osbourne."

Wrong, he was trying to make me look like some shrivelled sixty-two-year-old has-been. I couldn't exactly say that, though.

"I like Ozzy Osbourne," I objected instead.

"So do I. But if I thought for second I looked like him, I'd shoot myself."

He had a point, but then, if I thought for a second I looked like *him*, ginger curls and all, it'd be a race to see who got to the gun first.

"Can I have a look?" I asked.

"No, not until I've finished."

I toyed with the idea of jumping out of the chair and running into the bathroom anyway, but he'd probably bring me down like a wounded wildebeest before I was halfway across the rug. So I stayed and looked at the mounds of hair on the floor around the chair – there seemed to be so *much* of it! – with the kind of dumb misery you usually only see on the face of very small children who realize they've wet their pants and don't know how to tell the teacher without dying of embarrassment.

Sara came in with a tray and gave a squeal when she saw me.

"What?" I said. "What?" and sat up as if I'd been jabbed in the back with a machete.

Monsieur Alexander pressed me back into the chair with the ease of a mastodon felling a sapling.

"Have something to drink," he said. "Then we'll do your face."

I took a healing mouthful.

"So," I said to the Ginger Furball. "How come 'Monsieur' Alexander? You may be able to pass that off as a French accent round here, but it doesn't convince me."

His eyebrows shot up like a fun-fur roller blind. Then he grinned.

"My father was French," he said. "But I grew up in Wigan."

Well, that explained a lot.

"You can call me Alec."

"Everyone calls me Kat."

Everyone except Noni, that is. Alec and Kat. It had a certain ring to it, like a naff comedy duo.

"You don't have a French accent."

He shrugged.

"People seem to like my accent as it is."

I found that hard to believe. Listening to him made my whole personality hurt. OK, so I may be a snotty southern cow, but Wigan? That's not an accent, that's a speech impediment.

He put his glass back on Sara's tray.

"Enough of that," he said. "Time for me to be at that face of yours."

Ah yes, that face of mine. Soon to be somebody else's. I tried to smile.

The face wasn't much of an issue. He gave me a mini-facial: cleanse, scrub – all that stuff you never normally bother with. At least, you never bother with if you're me. If you're Sadie, it's the kind of ritual you pursue with utter devotion based on a deep fear that if you neglect it even for one day, the gods will strike you dead. Or at least give you spots. (Sadie sometimes gets spots anyway, which shows how evil and ungrateful the gods can be.) I asked him if I was going to have to have a whole new complexion, complete with stick-on latex wrinkles, but he gave me A Look worthy of Noni, and said, "Your grandmother doesn't have wrinkles." I thought that was about as likely as the Pope not knowing the words to the Lord's Prayer, but all I said was, "Don't you mean, Noni doesn't *do* wrinkles?" to which he said "No, *I* don't do wrinkles," and proceeded to give my eyebrows the tweezing of their life. By the time he'd finished I had tears running down my face and my forehead felt as if it had just had a close encounter with a flame-thrower. I must have hurt his professional pride with the wrinkle jibe. I made a mental note not to annoy him again. At least not while he had unlimited access to my nerve endings.

The next barrel of laughs was the outfit. I mean, seriously, me fit into any of Noni's stuff? This was where I was sure we would at last have to give up and call it a day. But no! (See above note on evil gods.) Sara appointed herself wardrobe mistress and hauled me off into a walk-in closet the size of my bedroom at home, where she swiftly and expertly removed my clothes and left me standing feeling exposed, vulnerable and nervous as hell. I trotted out my usual line in times of appearance-related stress: "I have no boobs."

She gave my chest a critical glance.

"I'm not surprised with that bra," was all she said, and whipped a tape measure off the back of the door. Yow, it was cold! "I'll order you a proper brassière."

Wow, there really were people who still said "brassière". I wondered what manner of garment this might be. Probably something excruciating designed by a sadist, with more underwiring than an electric train set. I remembered some graffiti I'd seen in one of the loos in the bar at my mom's college in Oxford – a real cry from the heart: "Darth Vader is alive and well and designing women's shoes." Or maybe she'd get me one of those Wonderbras. I'd always kind of fancied one of those. My mom said they were called Wonderbras because when you took them off you wondered where your boobs had gone. I suspected that in my case it would be because when I put it on, I'd end up wondering why I still didn't have any.

Sara hauled a slip off a hanger and flung it over my

head. It was rather pretty, but not exactly me: Katriona Shaw, a vision in lavender lace and, wait a minute – what were those shrivelled horror items she was holding up – stockings? Yikes!

If Darth Vader is into designing shoes, suspender belts (garter belts in Noni speak) are the work of Satan himself. I tried to object.

"You have to wear hose," Sara said. "Otherwise your legs will look too white."

"What about fake tan?"

Was that really me? Me asking to have my lower limbs painted bronze?

The door was opened and Monsieur A. was consulted.

"I can do that," I heard him say. "But I'll have to wax her legs first."

I was nearly fighting to get the stockings on after that. The tweezers had just about done it for me. And I still had bitter memories of removing that beastly beard every night of the school play.

Next came the dress: a neat, close-fitting little number in navy with white piping. I loathed it, but it was very Noni. Then Sara produced a swathe of chiffon and proceeded to muffle my head in several layers (so why bother with the haircut, huh?) The ensemble was, literally, topped off with a hideous coolie hat in navy straw. (I only know all this detail because Sara was giving me a running commentary through the whole ordeal.) Then the shoes: a pair of navy sandals with two-inch heels – straight from Monsieur Vader's Death Star collection.

"I can't walk in those," I protested. "I've never worn heels before!"

Sensing I was nearly ready and halfway decent, Al the Pal had appeared in the door.

"Well, you're going to have to learn," he said, unsympathetically. "Come on."

I tottered forwards, tripped over the runner for the sliding doors and fell into his arms.

"Steady on, flower," he said, propping me back up again and, like Jesus, commanding me to walk. "We can't afford to have you breaking your ankle as well."

As I reeled past him on what felt like acrobats' stilts, I couldn't help feeling that was the first sensible idea I'd heard all day.

Sara followed me, holding out a pair of sunglasses that would have done Dame Edna Everage proud.

"Put these on and turn round," she said. "You can look now."

I turned round, and saw … Noni.

For a moment I glared at her. What was she doing out of bed and why was she…? It was only the briefest of nano-seconds. You can do a lot of thinking in a nano-second. Then I had all the time in the world to realize my mistake. It *was* Noni. It *was*. It *was*. But, worse than that, it was also me. I was appalled. I looked at Sara, who was virtually hugging herself with delight. Then I looked at Alec. He was smiling quietly, confidently, as if he'd known how this would turn out all along.

"I hate you!" I said and put my hand over my mouth. Now I wasn't just appalled; I was scared.

"When you've quite recovered we can go back through," said Alec. "Noni will want to see you."

"No!"

He didn't say anything.

"She doesn't want to see me," I said. "She wants to see her."

"Then today's her lucky day."

I couldn't believe how calm he was. Monsieur stinking Alexander. My grandfather (my dad's dad, not Grandpa Zack) always said you couldn't trust the French, which I'd always thought totally racist and unfair. Now I began to see his point.

"Come on," said Sara, and scuttled over to open the door. I half expected her to shout "trick or treat". Alec put a hand in my back and exerted a gentle pressure forwards. I nearly fell over again. He caught my elbow. I glowered up at him through my Dame Edna specs.

"Remember," he said. "You can still say 'no'."

Oh thanks, Alec! Thanks for nothing! Thanks to him, saying "no" had just become a million times harder. But "no" it was going to have to be. Just because I did look like Noni, a bit – well, OK, a lot – didn't mean I could actually pass as her with someone who knew her, someone who'd actually spoken to her before. I held the thought, recovered my balance, tried to recover my wits and stomped towards the door. I caught my heel in the rug, but by now I was so angry that instead of falling over, I simply kicked it aside without breaking stride. How's *that* for a learning curve?

We made our entrance. Alec and Sara walked in first, hiding me behind them. (Sara wasn't exactly needed for this; you could have hidden at least three of me behind Alec and still had room for a small motor vehicle.) Through the crook of his elbow I could see Noni sitting up against the pillows, clutching Madge. Esteban, who'd been sitting by the bed flicking through a magazine, stood up. I felt sick. I felt exactly like I had before our first performance of *Twelfth Night*. Suddenly I needed the loo. Badly. Maybe that was the answer. Maybe I should simply wet myself. That should get me off the hook. Dodgy bladder. They wouldn't dare let me within tiddling range of Sam Schneider if they thought I had *that* problem.

Sara and Alec looked at each other, nodded and, with a loud "Ta-da!" sprang apart and there I was.

The reaction was mixed. Esteban shouted, "Jeez-us!" and hit his thigh with the magazine. But Noni simply stared. And stared. Then she put a hand to her mouth, and even I could see it was trembling.

"What do you think?" said Sara, excitedly. "Doesn't she look just like Audrey Hepburn?"

Which, given I was supposed to look like Noni, was kind of stupid, and kind of tactless too.

At last Noni spoke. She held out her hand to me (tremble, tremble) and said in a voice that was little more than a whisper, "Come here, my darling" and patted the side of the bed. I tottered over and sat down carefully, hoping my seams weren't about to split. She took my hand and looked at me, really looked at me – or rather, looked at the outside of me – for a long time. Then she said, quietly, "Oh my God, do I really look like that?" and began to cry.

My turn to shout "Jeez-us!"

I didn't. I was too busy hoping she was going to call the whole thing off. Dream on, Katriona. Instead, she turned an attractively tear-stained face to Alec and said, "But she's so beautiful."

???

"Of course she's beautiful, you daft bugger," he said. "She's your granddaughter. She's the image of you. I saw that the first time I met her."

Aha! So that explained the chin-grabbing, staring

routine he'd gone into when I'd bumped into him that first morning. And Rick. And Esteban, who I'd never set eyes on before, spotting me straight off at the airport. "Oh my God" just about summed it up.

I fell back on my usual line in times of crisis.

"But I have no boobs," I said.

This seemed to break the spell. Noni's eyes snapped to my chest.

"Of course you have boobs," she said. "They're just hiding."

Hiding? Now that was a new take on an old problem.

"I'm ordering her a new brassière," said Sara.

"Now wait a minute," I said. "Before anyone goes ordering anything, I still haven't said I'm doing this. And I'm not. No way. OK, so I can be made up to look like you. Fine. But that's not even the half of it. I would have to be you. I'd have to walk like you, talk like you; I'd have to be able to *think* like you. I can't do that."

"Nonsense." Noni was brisk now. "That's acting. You can do that. If I can, I know you can. You're a Waters."

"Er – reality check!" It was getting scary again. "*You* are a professional actress. *I* am just your average fifteen-year-old."

That struck a nerve. Noni drew herself up like a cobra that had just spotted a mongoose.

"You are my granddaughter," she said, enunciating every word as if it was some kind of elocution test. "You were wonderful in *Twelfth Night*. Your mother told me so."

Thanks, Mom!

"That?" I said. "That was the school play." And I tried to put the same sneer into "school" that I'd heard

106

her use. "We're talking me up on a stage with the audience watching from a safe distance. And even then they could see it was me. Even with the beard. They just didn't care."

"You don't know the first thing about it," said Noni. "Acting is an effort of will. The audience believes you are who you're pretending to be because they couldn't possibly believe anything else. It's like hypnotism. You make them believe it because you *will* it."

"No," I said. "You do, because you can. I can't."

"You can."

"I can't!"

"You will!"

"I won't!"

So there.

She looked as if she was contemplating throwing a scene (and when Noni threw a scene, a lot of other things usually got thrown as well.) I saw Madge's ears go back.

"Look," I said. "I really want to help you, Noni. I really do. But can't you see, it's crazy. You can't ask me to do this. It's not fair. I'll mess up and end up doing more harm than good. And I'll never forgive myself. I know you think I'm letting you down, but the truth is just the opposite: it's because I don't want to let you down. And I would. I know I would. Can't you just tell this guy you tripped and hurt your leg? Why is that such a big deal? It was an accident. So?"

She seemed to shrivel in front of me. Her shoulders sagged and her head drooped.

"You're right," she said, at last. "I'm sorry, Katriona. I should never have asked you even to do this much. Do forgive me, darling. It's just that…" Her voice trailed away expressively, then, at exactly the right moment, strengthened again. "Well, never mind." She sat up again and smiled bravely. "I'll have to call Sam and explain. I'll do it tomorrow."

"I'm sure he'll understand," I said, now feeling totally awful about the whole thing.

"I doubt it," she said. "He's very superstitious about actors having accidents. He has a history of stars falling ill or injuring themselves. He thinks he's jinxed. Silly, really. So I know how he'll react. But, never mind. You're right. We'll have to try and think up something else. Or I'll have to accept the movie was not to be. After all, I don't need to work any more. But it would have been nice. One more picture."

She sighed expressively and patted me on the knee.

"You can go and change now," she said. Another brave smile. "Oh my, when I saw you like that, I couldn't believe my eyes."

Feeling like the world's biggest worm, I stood up. She made a dismissive gesture and pressed her lips together. The hand had stopped trembling, I noticed, but now her chin looked suspiciously wobbly. I turned and stumbled for the door. I could have blamed the heels, but in fact my own eyes had suddenly gone all misty. I guess it was the sunglasses.

When I came back out as me, everyone was being artificially cheerful. No one would look me in the eye.

"Your mother called to let you know they've arrived," Sara said, biting her lip as if gnawed by inner demons. "She's calling back in five minutes."

It was an excuse to get out of there and away from all those understanding, but oh-so-pained eyes. I mumbled something about going to wait for it in my room and headed for the door. As I left, Noni tossed another burning ember onto the coals of fire

108

already piled high on my head.

"Darling," she said, brightly. "I do want to you to know how much I appreciate what you did. Thank you for trying."

Her smile was like a dagger in my heart.

I fled.


My mother sounded as if she was sitting in a metal dustbin on the back side of the moon.

"Hello sweetie!" she shouted. Shouting didn't seem to help much. "We're here."

"Where?"

"The hotel. In Georgia."

"What's it like?"

"I don't know. It's dark outside."

I tried to do a quick mental calculation of the time difference and failed.

"How are you, sweetie?"

"Fine. How are you and Dad?"

"OK, tired. Not a good journey. How's Noni?"

Hmm. How *was* Noni?

"Um, she's OK. She twisted her ankle a bit yesterday, but she's fine, really."

Not. Not. NOT!!!

"How's she been about Karl?"

Karl? Karl? My brain went into overdrive. Oh – Karl! Noni's terminally ex ex.

"Er, fine. She hasn't mentioned him."

A blizzard of metallic rustling ensued as if my mum had found some old kitchen foil at the bottom of the bin and was rolling about in it looking for leftovers. We tried talking more, but the noise defeated us. We screamed our goodbyes and took our leave of Georgia's answer to British Telecom.

When I finally plucked up the courage to emerge,
Monsieur Alexander had gone and Sara told me Noni
was asleep. I went and swam in the pool for a bit, but
my heart wasn't in it. No Pool God. Then I went back
inside and flicked through the channels on the TV.
Nothing. At least 600 channels and nothing worth
watching. I went back up to my room. Now what?
OK, maybe Pool God may have taken his glorious self
elsewhere, but ... I had Jamie's number. I picked up the
piece of paper I had written it down on and looked at
the phone. It was no good. I just couldn't do it. I didn't
dare. What was I supposed to say to him? More to the
point, what was he going to say to me? Especially after
... after...

OK, time to reveal my deepest shame. You may
think I was being a total wuss about the whole Noni
thing, but what you don't know is that I had already
done my bit as a character actress. The result: absolute
and utter humiliation. I've been holding out on you so
far. I mean, who wants to talk about that kind of
embarrassment, especially when boys are involved,
especially boys like Jamie, but I guess I'm going to have
to tell you about it sometime, and now seems as good a
time as any. Brace yourselves: it's about as bad as it can
get.

And then some.

110

WILLIAM SHAKESPEARE'S BRILLIANT COMEDY OF DISGUISE
AND MISTAKEN IDENTITY (RING ANY BELLS?), *TWELFTH
NIGHT*.
LOCATION: THE NORTH OXFORD HIGH SCHOOL FOR
GIRL'S* MAIN HALL

*Note: the North Oxford High School for Girls. Of course,
Shakespeare didn't use female actors. So we were following tra-
dition in that cross-dressing thing, only were crossing it the
other way. So instead of that "boys dressed as girls dressed as
boys" routine – ha ha! – we had girls dressed as girls dressed as
boys – ha ha ha! It kind of worked.

I could hear my dad somewhere in the third row. He
has this really loud, snorty laugh which can be quite
embarrassing, but when you're on stage trying to be
funny, it really helps to feel the audience is getting the
jokes as well. And we were funny. I know we were. I
could just feel it. Which is why Shakespeare is such a
genius. How old is that play? Four hundred years and
counting, and it still makes you laugh out loud. I
almost wished Noni could have been there. Almost.

Afterwards, before we'd scraped off all the make-up
and hung up those bloomers and ruffs for the last time,
Toby Belch (aka Claire Smailes – a short, stout, large-
busted lass) and I tottered out to receive the adulation
of an adoring public. Or at least of our adoring fami-
lies. Claire's little sister was dancing round us, pulling
at our costumes and trying to see how they fastened –
or unfastened. She can be a bit of a brat.

"You look so funny," she said. "Your face is so
white and yours is so red, and you're both all sweaty!"

Not what you really want to hear from a fan. For
some reason this fetching description made my dad

111

produce the family camera and insist we pose for some gruesome shots.

"Last chance to catch you girls in full costume!"

We put our arms round each other, pulled faces, posed and generally played the brilliant comediennes we now knew we were; and I was just thinking, Thank God this is an all-girls event, when a voice said, "Hi there!" and it was Jamie.

Oh great. There I am dressed like a prat in wrinkly tights and puffy panties looking like an advert for adult incontinence pants, I'm sweating like a pig, and I've just been making the world's stupidest faces, and who should appear but a guy I only got to meet once before, but who I would really like to have got to know a bit better before he found out I'm a raving nutcase with a nice line in historical cross-dressing.

And I don't think I'd mentioned the beard either, had I? Not on him, on me. I had a wispy bit of beard stuck on the end of my chin that waggled up and down when I talked. Great for amusing the punters. Not so great for impressing your average guy. Not on a girl, anyway.

He had the good manners not to say anything out loud, but I could see his eyes drifting down to the tights and then back up to the beard.

"Oh, hi there!" I said as casually as I could, as if I dressed like this all the time and it was no big deal. It came out as a squeak.

My mom swivelled round to check out the new-comer.

"Well, hello," she said. "Kat, sweetie, who is...? Do we know...?"

I hate it when she goes all coy and starts simpering. Those Waters genes putting in a rare appearance.

"This is Jamie," I said, beard waggling merrily. "He's moving here from Dull, I mean Hull."

"Hello there!" my dad said, all heartily, and – oh cringe! – he stuck out a hand. Jamie looked totally taken aback, but made a nice recovery and shook it. I suppose after the costume horror, this must have seemed quite normal. His hair kind of flopped over one eye, which was sort of cute. In an ordinary guyish kind of a way. Ish. At my elbow I was aware that Claire seemed to be inflating her boobs. Neat trick, except it made her look like a zeppelin.

"Were you here for the play?" my mom asked.

Oh please, God, no. Although it was unlikely he was here solely on the basis of a rumour that there were hot chicks with facial hair putting on a show at the girls' school.

"Yeah, my sister will be coming here next year and my parents got tickets."

"Did you enjoy it?" – Dad.

"I thought it was great. Really funny."

Well, he was hardly going to say it sucked like a vacuum cleaner in front of my folks, was he? He gave me kind of a knowing look and grinned.

"You were really funny," he said. "A woman of many talents."

I don't think he was being totally sarcastic, and he did say "woman". Not "creature" or "pervert". A pervert of many talents. When I finally apply to university, I shall make sure that goes on the first page of my CV.

"How d'you manage to do the whole guy thing?" he said.

Suddenly I found myself wishing desperately it hadn't been too convincing.

"You were really convincing."

Damn!

"Oh," I said airily, trying to sound as if it was something I did all the time. "It's all about pretending you're not actually who you really are. Kind of like making yourself disappear." Not good. That just made it out to be some kind of conjuring trick. He'd be expecting me to produce a rabbit from my codpiece next. "I mean, you have to forget about being you and concentrate on being the character. So, if you're playing a man ..."

I could see my beard wagging and tried not to look at it. The last thing I needed now was to develop a prize squint.

"... you have to think that's what you are. You have to believe you're a man."

Wag wag wag.

He was really grinning now. God, did I really come out with all that pretentious rubbish?

"I'll have to try it sometime," he said.

Oh, ha ha! Ha! Ha! Hee!

I think it must have been the nerves. I could feel myself starting to get hysterical again.

Hee hee hee!

Stop it, Kat!

But my dad thought that was pretty funny too and he did his snorty thing, and then Claire started up, but just as it looked like it was going to turn into Katriona Shaw's Academy of Laughter, two other relatively normal-looking grown-ups appeared, introduced themselves as Jamie's parents and hauled him away. Not a moment too soon, except I feared the damage was done by then. At least he seemed kind of reluctant to go. He looked back over his shoulder as he disappeared into the throng.

114

"I like the beard," he said. "D'you grow it yourself?"
Then he was gone.

In the brief silence that followed, all I could hear was the slow hiss of Claire deflating her breasts again. It matched the hiss of the air rushing out of my ego.

END OF FLASHBACK.

So now you can see why I wasn't exactly in a hurry to speak to Jamie again. But then, he had actually bothered to find out where I lived and gone round to leave his number for me to call him. I gazed at the phone in an agony of indecision.

It was no good. Maybe tomorrow. Sometime when I was feeling stronger. Or simply more desperate. Right now I simply couldn't face it.

The memory of the play was fresh in my mind. If it hadn't been for the whole Jamie incident it would have been great! Why did he have to turn up when he did? I decided to try and blot the whole episode from my mind and concentrate on the positive. Like the acting. I had enjoyed that. I really had.

It was then that I remembered that book I had found. What was it again? And who was the guy with the weird name? I fished under the pillow. There he was: Sándor What's-his-name. OK, so he wasn't exactly Jamie, but he would have to do for now. I rolled onto my stomach and gave myself up to 1960s Hungarian drama theory.

Whoever said young people today can't make their own entertainment?

For a man whose surname read like the bottom line of the eye chart at the opticians, Sándor Keczkes was

115

pretty interesting. According to the blurb inside the back cover, he'd worked with Stanislavski (second to last line of the eye chart), who even I'd heard of (thanks to Mr Jeffries). His photo was even more interesting. He looked like ... well, imagine this: you take a perfectly respectable-looking gnome, trap his head in a set of heavy duty lift doors and then take a cricket bat to the bits still showing. This man's face made the Himalayas look like a gently rolling plain. Ugly doesn't come close. But so ugly he was fascinating. And I thought I had problems. I mean, who needs boobs if you have ears so big they can probably pick up alien transmissions from distant galaxies? I opened at the page I'd marked and read on.

"Acting is not merely a craft; acting is not even solely an art; it is an act of will: the will to convince yourself to be the character you are to portray, the will to convince yourself you are that character but, more importantly, the will to convince your audience it is so."

Now where had I heard that before?

I took in the rest of the chapter and closed the book. It was heavy stuff. Not the kind of material you could take in at one sitting. I tucked the book back under the pillow and sighed. I was getting hungry. What were the chances of getting something to eat? Would I ever be allowed to eat here again, having failed so spectacularly to step up to the mark and do my bit for Noni? It was a risk I had to take. I mean, once I got inside the kitchen, Sara wasn't exactly going to wrestle me away from the fridge, was she? And if she tried, I knew I could call on untapped reserves of strength when it came to handling anything that got in the way of me and the food I knew was rightfully mine.

I was halfway along the landing, moving softly but with determination, when I heard a noise coming from Noni's room. I paused, expecting to hear the rhythmic hee-haw of her voice at rest (known to the rest of the world as "snoring"), but this was different: rhythmic, but subdued and hiccuppy. Noni, I realized with an unpleasant start, was crying.

I tiptoed over to the door and listened.

Yes, there was no mistaking it now. Behind the door, muffled, but unmistakeable, came the sound of weeping. Now what was I supposed to do? My stomach was saying, "Run a mile, and preferably in the direction of food." My heart was urging me to go and check on her. My brain had ceased functioning sensibly a long time ago. I decided to follow my heart. My stomach could wait. For now. Besides, hadn't I spotted a huge bowl of fruit in there on that adorable little table near the window only this morning? Maybe I could snag a banana while I was making sure she was OK.

I pushed open the door and went in.

Noni was curled up on her side, her face obscured in a mound of bedclothes, and she was sobbing quietly, but with real commitment.

I went over and sat on the edge of the bed.

"Noni?"

Sob.

"Noni?" Louder.

Louder sob.

I put my hand on what I guessed was her shoulder.

"Noni, it's me."

The bedclothes heaved and a small pink face emerged, sniffed and gulped. For a moment I thought it was Madge. I half expected her to lick my hand.

"Are you OK?" I said. Dumb question of the year. Do sixty-two-year-old women usually sob into their Ralph Lauren bed-linen when they're OK?

A hand emerged and took mine. Softly. Not the hammer-thrower grip I was usually treated to.

"Katriona..." Snuffle. Snuffle. "I don't want you to see me like this."

You and me both, lady. I gave her hand an encouraging squeeze.

"What's the matter?"

Dumb question of the year number two.

"Nothing, darling. Nothing."

Matching dumb answer.

"Is it the Sam Schneider thing?"

More snuffling and what could have been a nod. Or a twitch. Or a minor seizure.

I didn't know what to say.

"I'm sorry."

"You mustn't be. It's not your fault."

Which is not how it was feeling to me right then.

She rolled onto her back, winced, and looked at the ceiling. I guessed her ankle must be hurting.

"I should have known better," she said. "When Sam first called, I should simply have said 'no'." A sigh. "I have to accept, I'm not the woman I was."

Now this was heresy. OK, so I hadn't always seen as much of Noni as I might (not that that was my fault either) but I had known her all my fifteen years and if anything else had changed, she hadn't. Noni – and Grandpa Zack – were like nature's constants: they might get older, but they never essentially changed.

"Of course you are," I said. "And then some."

A smile appeared amid the tears.

"You really think so?"

118

"Of course I do!"

"I'm fifty-seven, you know."

Er, make that sixty-two, Rip van Winkle.

"So?"

She seemed to consider this.

"Hey," I said, struggling to find the script. "Whatever happened to the sexual power of the older woman?"

That threw her. I saw her pause, cast me a surprised glance and then stop and think. Mistake. I thought she was going to burst into tears all over again.

"I don't know," she whispered. "I really don't know."

And she began to cry again, quietly, almost as if she wasn't even aware of it herself. I sat there, holding her hand, not knowing what to say.

"Can I tell you something, darling?" she said at last. "I've never told anybody else. It's always been one of those memories you have just for you. But I remember once, when I was a girl – young, not a teenager like you, but still a girl – my mommy and daddy – your great-grandparents – took me to the beach. We didn't have a lot of money then and we didn't get to go out much, so it was something special. I remember everything about it: the smell of the sea, the feel of the sand. And I remember they'd bought me a new bathing suit. It was red with little white ruffles, and I thought it was the prettiest thing I'd ever seen. I was so proud I hardly wanted to go into the sea and get it wet.

"We were there all day. And then finally Poppa called to me to come back because we were going home, but I didn't want to go. Not yet. But I knew I had to. And I was standing there in the sea, watching the setting sun

119

send this river of light across the water to where I was standing. And suddenly I had one of those moments when everything becomes absolutely clear and you understand things you usually never even think about. And I remember looking at the sun and the sea and my little red and white bathing suit and thinking, 'Here I am, me. I know I'm only ten, and when I grow up ten won't seem so very old. But I know who I am now. I'm already me. And, even when I grow up, this is who I'll always be.' And, do you know, I've never forgotten that. I know I must look like a sad old woman to you, because you're so young and you have your whole life ahead of you. But I've always remembered that day on the beach in Jersey, and, believe it or not, I'm still that little girl. The way I look on the outside may have changed, but inside I'm still the woman I always was."

She was crying properly again now.

"I'm sorry," she said. "I don't expect you to understand that."

But, funnily enough, although I kind of didn't, in a way I did.

I squeezed her hand.

"It's OK," I said. "You're special. You always have been."

She sighed with her whole body.

"You too, darling," she said. "Thank you for being here with me this summer. I was so afraid you weren't going to come." Pause. Gulp. "I do love you so much."

Oh boy, this was really overdoing it. I writhed like a bag of eels.

"I love you too," I said.

OK, what was I supposed to say? And, anyway, I meant it. Yes, I did. Like that little girl standing in the waves on the Jersey shore, I realized I did love Noni. It

120

didn't mean I didn't think she was crazy and ridiculous and difficult and ... and ... and... But she was my grandmother. And Grandpa Zack had loved her enough to marry her and have my mom. And that was enough to make her special for me.

"Noni," I said. And I can only think the whole situation had made me temporarily insane. "Forget what I said earlier. I'll do it. I will. I promise you. I'll talk to Sam Schneider. Really I will. And even if I do mess up, what do we have to lose?"

What indeed?

Only our sanity.

So what? I've come to realize sanity is overrated. But then, I would say that, wouldn't I, because I'm obviously mad as an owl.

It's those Waters genes.

LOCATION: PALM DESERT
TIME: SEVERAL HOURS LATER

We held a council of war that evening: Noni, Esteban, Sara, Monsieur Alexander (yes, he came back – did that man have no life?) and me. Noni tried to make a speech about how noble and selfless I was being, but I wasn't having any of it. I was already getting cold feet again and starting to regret my moment's fatal weakness. Being told I was a heroine didn't impress me at all when all I felt like was a prize idiot. It had been an entirely emotional response to the sight of Noni crying. If my brain had checked in instead of being off somewhere where the buses don't run, I would have stuck with patting her hand and saying "There, there". Instead I was now officially signed up for the summer's latest big event: the ultimate humiliation of Katriona. It sounded like a movie already: rating – 15; category – horror.

Surprisingly, while Sara and Esteban seemed totally enchanted with the whole idea, it was Lancashire's answer to Chewbacca, the chief architect of the whole sad scheme, who offered me one last chance to escape.

"Are you sure about this?" he said. "You can still change your mind, you know."

Noni made a gargling noise. I thought she was about to swallow her tongue or bring up a furball. I glared at him.

"Absolutely not," I said. The big ginger git. Couldn't he see that when Noni Waters's granddaughter said she was going to do something, it was as good as done? I'm not sure this was actually true, but I was already struggling to think like Noni. (This hurt my brain, which had at last returned home and was no doubt wondering what on earth had happened while it was away. Ha! Serve it right for deserting me when I needed it most.)

"We already know Katriona can look like me..." Noni was saying.

As if that was all that really mattered.

"Excuse me," I said. "But what's scaring me isn't looking like you." (Not that that wasn't scary enough.) "It's *being* you."

She seemed unperturbed.

"I've thought of that," she said. "And I've asked Sándor Kezckes to come and work with you. He's my old drama coach."

Light dawned. The Hungarian gnome! So that was how you pronounced his name: Kez-kiz.

"You won't have heard of him, darling, but he is simply the best..."

Time for me to claw back some self-respect.

"Actually," I said. "If you mean the Sándor 'Kez-kiz'

who wrote *Acting Against Character*, I have."

Noni actually stopped in mid-sentence and looked at me with what I liked to think was admiration. Still, it wouldn't hurt to make sure.

"I've read it."

(Half of it, anyway.)

She looked impressed.

"Well now, I am impressed," she said.

See.

"You mean, he's still alive?"

She shoved out one of those musical laughs.

"Of course! He's quite elderly now, almost ninety, but still absolutely one hundred per cent up here." She tapped her forehead. Good, at least there would be one person involved who still had all their marbles, even if it was a Hungarian goblin who was older than God.

Noni gave her forehead another tap with a perfectly manicured nail to emphasize her point. Or maybe it just felt good. That nail! It was long and tapered and blood red. Oh no! That meant I was going to have to get mine done. I look down at my stumpy finger-ends. Yes, folks, confession time: I'm a confirmed nail biter. Oh well, one more challenge for Wigan Man.

Now I was aware Noni was looking at me in that way adults do when they want to tell you something they know you're going to hate, but they're going to force on you anyway.

"Total immersion," she said, like some Baptist minister spying an unwholesome new convert. "It's the only way for you to get properly into character."

OK. I mean, what was I doing right now if not closely watching every move she made?

"When you go to bed tonight, you go to bed as me. When you get up, you get up as me. You go through

123

the day as me. And that means everything: clothes, shoes, everything. The whole look."

"What?"

"You'll need the time to learn to walk in heels," Alec put in. Helpfully.

Cheek! But they were right. Even I could see that. I should have thought of it before. Oh great. My one-day nightmare facing down Sam Schneider had just had two days of hell tacked on up front for good measure. I tried not to scowl. Or at least to scowl like Noni: with my ears. Then I spotted a possible silver lining to this otherwise all-encompassing cloud.

"Does this mean we get to swap rooms?" I said.

This time the Noni-scowl didn't mess around, but kicked straight in between the eyebrows. I just smiled. Sweetly.

I did not get the master suite. What I got was homework and plenty of it. Fortunately it was in a subject I knew well: film history. Noni sent me and Sara off to the study with a list of books, and she spent the rest of the evening lecturing me on Sam Schneider, Jack Winemaker and her own career on the silver screen. I think she was surprised I knew so much. Pleased too. It's all very well saying "I love you, Noni", but when you can reel off the co-stars, the director and the producer of every film she ever made (even the early bad ones), that has to mean something. So far so good. I looked the part and, as long as Sam Schneider didn't ask me to move or speak, but simply set me a written quiz on Hollywood: 1960 to the Present Day, we were in business. At least I'd learned one new thing about him: he was short-sighted. OK, it wasn't much – blind, deaf and stupid would have been more helpful –

but it was something.

When she finally let me go to bed, my head was spinning. While I was cleaning my teeth I looked at the new me in the mirror. OK, I had to admit, Alec had done a pretty good job with the hair. I tilted my head sideways and let the line brush across the point of my jaw. Not so bad after all. And I could see he was right about the parting. The parting. *The Parting*. Noni's 1977 hit directed by Tommy de Salle in which she starred opposite Adam Quincy. Yeesh! This was getting ridiculous. At this rate I would be waking up screaming titles, dates and cast lists every hour on the hour.

Somebody was waiting for me on the bed. Not Pool God (be still my beating heart). Madge.

"Hey, you," I said. "Don't tell me you think I'm Noni."

She wagged her tail.

"Traitor," I said.

She yawned.

"Go to sleep," I said. "We both have a lot of work to do – when the morrow comes."

(*When the Morrow Comes* – director: Jack Winemaker; co-star: Bill Norton; producer: Sam Schneider. Not one of Noni's best.)

In case you were wondering.

Location: Palm Desert
Time: Day one of the Great Katriona Shaw Makeover Disaster

The morrow came all too soon. With it came: 1) Sara bearing breakfast – good; 2) Alec bearing That Case – bad; 3) Sara, again, with Noni-wear – horrible; and

**125**

4) at around 11 o'clock, Esteban bringing Sándor Keczkes from LA – the jury was still out on that one. By then I was in full Noni regalia including false nails, a matching lipstick in what I can only describe as harlot red, and another pair of appalling sandals.

The front door opened.

"That must be Sándor," said Noni, who by now appeared to be highly delighted with the whole situation. "Go down and greet him, darling. I want to see if he thinks you're me."

She made it sound like she was offering me the treat of my life. Surprised to see me hesitate instead of immediately bounding from the room with cries of joy and enthusiasm, she waggled her hands at me impatiently. There were voices downstairs now.

"Well, go on!" she said.

I went.

Sándor Keczkes was not like his photograph.

Much.

I realized as soon as I saw him that the Sándor K. gracing (if that's the right word) the back cover of *Acting Against Character* had been a much younger man. On top of this, the photographer, God bless him or her, had used all the art at their disposal to disguise the full impact of their subject when viewed live and in the flesh. The creature that hobbled through the front door that fine summer morning appeared to be approximately one metre high and had no head. I was crouched at the top of the stairs peering through the rail with a view to checking him out before I made my move. A move I wasn't planning to make any time soon, until I was satisfied the life form currently infesting what Noni pleased to call the "atrium" was at least

126

vaguely humanoid. And humanoid definitely included a head. This character looked like something that had escaped from the *Star Wars* special effects lab.

Then he turned round. Aha! A head! OK so it appeared to be growing out of the middle of his chest, but there was no mistaking those ears. He was, I now realized, simply so old and bent he couldn't have stood up straight if he'd tried. Shame. He could have done with the extra height. Sara was fussing around trying to help him remove his coat and wasn't having a very easy time of it, coats generally being designed to fit human-shaped people with all their arms and legs in the usual places. Seeing them both occupied with this, I decided to make an appearance.

What would Noni do now? Easy. Noni would float down the stairs holding out both hands like some demented sleepwalker trilling cries of welcome and delight. But then Noni was used to navigating in nine-inch spike heels. Noni could probably have breezed through an SAS assault course in stiletto mules. These were skills I had yet to master. Actually I'd found the heels weren't so bad – so long as I didn't actually try and walk in them. Any kind of movement brought on an instant attack of altitude sickness marked by nose-bleeds, frantic arm waving and terminal staggering. Not likely to impress Mr K. Unless he was used to Noni's drinking habits, of course. I abandoned the idea of the gracefully extended hands, gripped the rail as if my life depended on it (which it did) and eased onto the first step.

Ker-lunk.

How come when Noni walked in these things, she only ever made a light clicking noise? I sounded like an all-in wrestler crossing a metal floor in steel-tipped clogs. But I could only worry about one thing at a time. Never mind the noise, what I needed was to concentrate on keeping my balance. I'd made it onto step one without incident. Only another eleven or so to go.

Ker-lunk.

Ker-unk.

Pause.

KER-LUNK!

Help!

Ker-lunk-lunk-lunk.

Nearly there.

Ker-lunk.

Ker-lang. (Ker-lang?)

Ker-lunk.

I could feel my palms growing sweaty on the rail. The Hungarian humanoid was watching my descent with some interest.

Two steps to go.

I needed a break. I stopped, let go of the rail and held out both hands. Resisting the temptation simply to pitch headfirst to the bottom, I stood up straight, stuck on a gracious smile (or what I hoped was a gracious smile) and warbled, "Welcome!"

The gnome appeared to tilt his head. Bright eyes flashed centre-chest.

"Vere's Noni?" he said.

OK, so I had been the one complaining it wouldn't work, but I still felt crushed. I teetered there for a moment, still smiling in some forlorn hope that this would restore the illusion (such as it was), then I simply gave up and sat down on the stairs before my ankles snapped like twigs. I felt something small but essential rip horribly close to my bum.

"She's upstairs," I said. "She can't walk."

The gnome gave a chuckle. Like they do. He sprang up onto the bottom step with astonishing agility and patted my hand.

"And you must be Katriona," he said. More twinkling from those button eyes.

"Yes," I said, miserably. "But everyone calls me Kat."

Now he patted my cheek, his fingers warm and hard and dry, just like Grandpa Zack's.

"Zen let us go and see her, zat naughty girl," he said. "So much trouble she gives us. But ve vill sort her out, you and I. Yes?"

I looked into that face. That face! And saw all the things I had needed to see since this whole mad scheme had first reared its ugly head. I saw sympathy and I saw understanding. Sándor Keczkes might look like a relief map of the Andes, but Sándor Keczkes also looked like an ally; Sándor Keczkes, I realized, was a friend.

He was holding out his hand to me now. I took it and levered myself back to my feet. Standing one step up from him, I virtually had to bend my neck ninety degrees to see the top of his head.

"Er ... you'd better come up, then," I said.

The head appeared to nod. An arm emerged beneath it. Fingers waggled.

"After you, my dear," he said.

We clumped into Noni's room looking like a couple of newly-weds from *The Munsters*. Hello, Noni. Out came the hands, up went the chin and off she went at full warble. All she needed was a little ladder to run up and a bell to peck at the top.

"Sándor! Darling!"

If I had expected Sándor darling to sidle over to the bed (he had a strange sideways gait, like a crab) and offer himself up to be pecked instead, I was disappointed. Instead he simply flapped a hand at her and said, "Vot is zis nonsense you haf dreamed up?"

Vot indeed?

"Oh, Sándor, darling, it isn't nonsense. Not really. Not when you understand."

He was unimpressed.

"Nonsense!"

Noni started to pout.

"You're the only one who can help me."

"Zis is true."

"Will you? Darling. For me? For old times?"

For a woman who had probably never handled a trowel in her life (except to apply her make-up), she was laying it on pretty thick.

"If I do it at all," he said, "it will be for zis young vooman. She needs my help more zan you."

Hey, I was a vooman! I thought about that. It felt good.

"Now, ve vill eat and discuss vot has to happen."

A man after my own heart. I mean, who can think on an empty stomach?

Noni pressed a button by her bed to activate her Sara-tracking device. The gnome squinted up at me. He seemed to expect some kind of input.

"Lunch sounds good to me," I said. "But there's not a whole lot to discuss. Noni wants me to meet Sam Schneider and pretend to be her so he'll give her a part in his movie."

Simple really.

"I can't do it," I said. "But I've promised I'll try."

I thought he ought to know what he was up against.

He was already ambling towards the door. Actually he appeared to be ambling towards the far corner, but he was in fact moving doorwards.

"You may be surprised," he said. "I do not sink you know yet vot you can do."

Maybe not. But I had a pretty good idea. Vooman, I might be; world-class Noni impersonator, I was not.

But I could do food: one essential constant in an uncertain world. I cranked up the heels and reeled after him.

I could have saved myself the effort. We met Sara on the landing and she told us she was serving lunch on the roof terrace. This was Noni's idea, so she could be wheeled out to join us. It was the full line-up: me, Noni, Sándor, Alec, Esteban and Sara (when she wasn't zotting about serving good things). But then, everyone was in on this and everyone had a part to play. Everyone knew what they had to do and everyone knew they could do it. Except me.

Over to Sándor.

"Ve do not have so very long," he was saying. I knew it was him talking by the accent. I couldn't actually see him behind his bowl of salad. And that was after Sara had brought him two extra cushions. "Ve must vork continuously to prepare."

Oh good. Continuous work. And in heels too. Exactly the holiday I would have chosen for myself. I plucked fretfully at the scarf, which tickled my ears and made my head itch.

"Do I have to wear this?" I asked. Start with one of the easy problems and work up.

"Yes," said Noni.

I looked at Alec. He shrugged and looked at Sándor.

"If zis is how you vill be to meet Mr Schneider, zen, yes, you must vork viz zat."

No point asking about the shoes, then.

A small commotion behind the salad. Through a gap in the endive I could see him rummaging about in a tatty old briefcase on his lap.

"If we are to vork togezzer viz success, you must know my methods."

I guessed he was talking to me.

"I have brought you my book to read."

Surprise!

"Would that be *Acting Against Character*?" I said, smugly. "I've read it. Most of it, anyway."

That got his attention. At least, his ears looked suddenly alert.

"You have? Excellent! Zen ve can begin at vonce!"

What about dessert? I'd spotted a cheesecake the size of a wagon wheel earlier, and I wasn't giving that up in a hurry. Sara must have sensed my dismay, as she bobbed up and rushed it over to the table.

"Ho-kay, after ze cake," he conceded. Good, I didn't want to go on strike before I'd begun.

Noni didn't go for the fat and sugar fest, but opted for making an animal of herself with a dish of non-fat yoghurt and a handful of blueberries.

"I'm so looking forward to watching you two working together," she said, dabbing her lips. Two bright red smears appeared on the crisp white linen. I thought I saw Sara wince. I know I did.

It was going to be bad enough without having Noni calling out helpful suggestions from the sidelines like: "Don't stagger about like that, darling" or "I would *never* say that!"

132

I needn't have worried.

"No!" This was Sándor. "Maybe later, ven ve have achieved some progress. But, for now, ve must vork alone."

Thank you. Thank you!

Noni squeaked and objected, but he was adamant. Grandpa Zack would have approved.

Finally Sara cleared the table. Sándor stood up (it made him look shorter) and beckoned me to follow him. Esteban wheeled Noni back inside, and Alec followed them, apparently intent on carrying out some essential procedure on her feet and ankles. Like what? Strip-mining her toenails for minerals? Whatever he did, I hoped it would be, if not actually painful, at least uncomfortable. I didn't want to think I was going to be the only one being tortured out here.

The roof terrace followed the curve of the house. Sándor was already disappearing round the corner. I trotted obediently after him, wondering how two slices of weapons grade cheesecake could so quickly turn into a seething mass of butterflies.

And then the hiccups started.

I tottered after him, trying to control my breathing.

"So," he said, once we were out of sight of prying eyes. "How to begin?"

How indeed?

"If you have read my book, you vill know ze importance of ze vill. You must vill yourself into ze part and you must vill your audience to believe you are ze character you intend to be."

Which sounded all very easy put like that. The issue was: could I actually do it? I opened my mouth to point this out and a hiccup escaped. A loud one. Sándor looked at me critically.

133

"Are you quite vell?" he said.

Hic.

"I've got hiccups. Can I get a glass of water?"

He frowned. I hiccupped.

"No," he said. "Zis is a good exercise. You vill vill zem avay."

I thought I understood. I closed my eyes and thought about the hiccups. Encouraged by the attention, my body pushed out three good ones in a row.

"Not like zat! You cannot act viz your eyes closed!"

I could if I was pretending to be Sleeping Beauty.

"And you are concentrating in ze wrong direction!"

Hic.

"You are zinking about your hiccups. You should be zinking about your body wizout zem."

Aha!

Hic.

I tried again.

"Don't close your eyes!"

"Sorry."

Hic.

"Zink about ze vindow over zere. You believe you have seen someone looking out of it. You are curious. Ze house should be empty. You go over to see."

"You want me to walk over to that window?"

Hic.

He nodded.

"Without falling down?"

"Please."

OK. I could probably manage that. I launched myself towards it, Sándor shouting directions behind me.

"Be careful! You are a little afraid. You know some-one vishes you dead."

Hic hic hic!!!

"But you are curious. You stop for a moment and look. You are vondering."

I zig-zagged about a bit.

"Not vandering – vondering! You vonder who might be in there."

Oh, that kind of vondering! Well – duh! Actually, this was kind of fun. I crept up to the window, treading softly. Softly for me, that is. Sándor had gone quiet now. I took another small step. The assassin waited within. Hey, I was really getting into this now.

Hic.

Suddenly the window flew open. I screamed and fell sideways against the wall. Sara's head appeared.

"Sorry," she said. "I just wanted to ask if I could bring you something to drink while you were up here."

I clutched my chest and glared at her. How about a large sedative?

Sándor ambled over.

"Very good," he said.

I glared at him too.

"I'll bring you some water and some iced tea," said Sara and closed the window.

"She gave me the fright of my life," I said.

"Good. It vas because you had begun to believe in vat you vere doing. And – see – no more hiccups!"

He was right!

Actually, I thought it was the shock.

We got on pretty well after that. Sándor ran me through all kinds of exercises and he was good. He was amazing. The trouble was, I wasn't. Well, I was OK. So long as I was in imaginary situations with imaginary people. The minute I had to be Noni I went completely to pieces. I could feel myself getting hot and bothered and concentrating on all the wrong things. Sándor was beyond patient, but that only made me feel worse.

After an especially dismal effort at Noni-dom, Sándor suggested I go back inside to sit down and try to clear my mind. By now I had realized it wasn't just my mind that was the problem. By now I was in fear of my immortal soul. I just couldn't allow myself to be Noni. If I did, I was afraid that somehow I was going to disappear, and I would never come back.

I sat and fiddled with the hem of the dress. Today's number was another bum-hugger in white, with huge red poppies all over it. It sounds vile, but actually it was rather pretty. On the right person.

I knew Sándor was looking at me.

"Kat," he said. "You are such a clever young vooman."

That "vooman" again. I loved it.

"And you have real talent. Like your grandmuzzer."

But that was the problem. I wasn't like my grandmother. At all. Just because I could fit into her clothes, didn't make me her.

"Do you truly vant to do zis for her?"

Tough question, easy answer. I pulled even harder on the hem. If I'd had the matching ruby slippers I would have been slamming those heels together right now and screaming to get back to Kansas.

"No."

It was little more than a whisper.

"No?"

"Well, I do. Of course, I do. I mean, I want to help her. Just not like this. But I've said I'll do it now."

I looked at him miserably. He was balancing on the edge of an armchair, his little legs just touching the ground, the sunlight falling through the glass panels behind him catching his ears and making them glow translucent pink. He looked like Yoda.

"My dear," he said. "You must decide now. Eizer you vill do zis or not. If yes, zen you must vant it above all else."

"I don't want it. But I can't not."

"Is zat not also a form of vanting?"

I thought about that.

"I suppose so," I said slowly. "I don't want to do it, but I don't want not to do it either."

"Which is ze stronger desire in you?"

How about getting out of these stockings and unwrapping the Tutenkamen-inspired headgear for starters?

He hadn't finished.

"Vill you feel vorse if you do it or if you do not?"

Ah, now there was the million dollar question. And I still only had the fifty bucks Noni had given me and some spending money from my parents. I did my best.

"If I do it, I'll hate it," I said. "If I don't, I'll hate myself."

"Vich is vorse?"

Crunch time.

I looked at him. He spread his hands and smiled. I hate that whole Jedi thing. You just can't win.

"Let me say zis," he said. "To do it, you do not have to like it. But you must vant to do it enough to do it right. It is possible to vant something for reasons that are not only to do viz pleasure. It can even be for reasons vich are totally different from zat."

Like pain. He'd hit the nail on the head. He could hit me on the head next. What the hell? If it wasn't about pleasure, who cared?

I breathed hard a couple of times. Where were those hiccups when I needed them? I could have done with the distraction.

"OK," I said. "I want to do it."

"You vant to become Noni?"

"That's the whole point. No, I don't. I want to be able to make people think I'm her. That's different."

Now he was frowning. This was heresy and I knew it. It was one of the fundamentals of the Sándor Keczkes approach. He obviously thought so too, because he hopped off the chair and began to trundle about the room, cracking his knuckles together. He stopped for a moment, gave me a piercing look, and held up a finger. Then he was off again.

"First," he said. "Do not confuse 'vant' and 'vill'."

It was hard not to, the way he pronounced them.

"Take your emotions out of ze picture. You may not vant to be zis character. Whoever it is. Let us say you are to play an evil man. Let us say you are to play Hitler."

So what happened to the whole "vooman" number? OK, so it was a concept thing. I could handle that. But I couldn't see Hitler going across too well with Sam Schneider. Even Noni seemed preferable to that.

"Do you vant to be Hitler? No! Of course not! But you must play zis evil part so zat your audience believes, for zat time you are on ze stage, zat ze person zey see is zat man."

The zeds were flowing thick and fast. It sounded like he was talking through a swarm of bees.

"Zis is vat I mean by acting against character. To be a character so different you must renounce the character zat is essentially you."

Light began to dawn. Hey, this was good! I wish I'd

138

been taking notes. Mr Jeffries would have loved this. Time to show willing.

"So I don't have to want to be Noni, but I do have to will myself to be her?"

"Exactly."

Oh great! That had cleared that little problem up. Which just left the other one. The big one: how?

It's all very well talking about things. You can describe how to do something until you're blue in the face. You can even write it down. But then, when you actually have to do it, that's the real test. That was why I was always so useless at technology. I must be the only person alive to burn a salad. I made a wooden box no one has ever been able to open since. I put the zip in a pencil case backwards. Six times. But the absolute prize winner in the line up has to be the doorbell I designed and made last year. It looked great; it felt good. Even Mr Abrahams liked it. Until he pressed the button. In theory it should have lit up and played the theme tune to Indiana Jones. In theory. Instead, at the touch of the Abrahams finger, it made a loud farting noise and caught fire. Total disaster. OK, so I didn't think I was in any immediate danger of doing *that* in front of Sam Schneider, but there were any number of possibilities that had to come close.

Sándor had stopped revolving around the furniture like a top and was now standing beside my chair. I looked him in the eye, which was easy, as even sitting down I swear I was taller than he was.

"You need time to zink about zeez ideas by yourself," he said. "I vill go upstairs and talk to Noni. I vant you to go outside. Have some time alone. Valk about. Zink about being Noni. Calmly. Vizout emotion. It is a task. Zat is all. A difficult one, I know, but nozzing more. Smell ze flowers. Look around you. No one vill disturb you. Zis time is for you. Go and use it. Take as long as you like."

It really was beautiful out there. The light beckoned. The pool sparkled. OK, no swimming now. But maybe I could go for a dip later. A reward for good behaviour, perhaps. I stood up and tweaked the seat of the dress into place. (It was becoming instinctive now – even the heels weren't bothering me as much.) OK, I was Noni. Time to go explore the delights of my own little kingdom, and give the serfs hell if they dared get in the way. I pivoted on my heel (I *was* getting the hang of it) and made my exit.

LOCATION: PALM DESERT, THE GARDEN
TIME: TIME OUT

It was lovely out in the sun, the garden green against the pale gold of the desert beyond. And it was mine. I ambled about, head up, chest out – I do have boobs! I do have boobs! – smiling benignly at all I surveyed. I tried to remember what Sándor had said about pretending to be Hitler. Why Hitler of all people? But then I had a sneaking suspicion that if Hitler had had his evil way, Sándor Keczkes would not have lived to share his vision with the world. And it would have been a poorer place without him. The same was probably true for Sam Schneider as well. Hitler had a lot to answer for. He made Noni look like Mother Theresa.

I realized that I had begun talking out loud to myself, which was probably an early sign of the onset of madness, but as I was out here on my own, that was

OK. Except at about that moment there was a rustle behind me and an unknown voice said, "Excuse me?"

I must have set a new record for high jump from a standing position. So much for my solitary madness. I wasn't alone after all. I did that heel-pivoting thing again, only this time in an effort not to make things worse by falling over. A quick whirl of the arms and balance was restored. Now I was in a position to focus on the owner of the unknown voice.

It was Pool God.

He stood there, glorious, the sunlight forming a halo of gold around his bronzed bod.

"Excuse me?" he said.

I goggled at him. Thank God for the sunglasses. And why I'd ever complained about that scarf I did not know. Right then you could have shoved me into the latest fashion burka from the Ayatollah's spring collection and that would have been just fine by me.

"Miss Waters?"

Noni?

Where?

I was about to snap my head round in alarm when I realized just in time that he was talking to me. I tried to cover my confusion with a quick musical laugh. All that happened was a strange bubbling noise in my throat. Stop it! Stop it! The bubbling ceased. Good. What emerged in its place was a single, high-pitched uncanny squeak. Bad! BAD!!!

"That's me," I squealed. "I'm Miss Waters. Of course I am. Ha ha!" A laugh? Kind of. Musical? Definitely not. "Who else would I be?"

Then my voice packed up altogether.

He was holding his pool cleaning/straining/whatever-it-was kit. His hands looked strong and skilful.

"Oooh!"

"Miss Waters?"

Damn! I hadn't meant that one to pop out aloud either. Keep it simple. Keep it safe.

Resisting an overwhelming urge to fall at his feet and start moaning "I am not worthy," I merely smiled. Lipstick cracked in the corners of my mouth. Yuk! It was probably all over my teeth as well.

Don't lick your teeth! Do *not* lick your teeth!

And don't try to lick his teeth either.

"Yes?"

"Are you all right?"

No! NO! NO!!!

"Of course."

An awkward pause.

"I've come to do the pool."

"Of course."

Not very original, but the last one seemed to have caused no lasting damage.

He stood for a moment, obviously waiting for me to say or do something else. Like what? "Would you mind very much waiting while I drown myself in it first?" Or maybe I should just lie down and roll quietly away into the bushes. That way he was bound not to follow me.

What would Noni do? Probably wave an imperious hand and tell him to get on with it.

I opened my mouth.

Hic!

Not now! Not again!

"Are you sure you're all right?"

He looked genuinely concerned now, and a little nervous.

142

Oh no! He thought I was drunk. Obviously. I would if I were him.

"Excuse me," I gargled from behind my hand. "Hiccups."

I tried again.

Hic.

"Indigestion. Too much cheesecake at lunch. I need a glass of water."

He took a step nearer. Yikes! He looked so gorgeous I could smell it coming off him: the scent of gorgeous.

"Would you like me to get it for you?"

Yes. No!

He took another step towards me.

Whoa! Hold it right there, mister!

Now I took a step back. No problem, except there was a pool lounger right where I was least expecting it. It caught me behind the knees and I sat down on it with a yelp. Pool God sprang forwards. At about the same time and with the same velocity I sprang upwards. We collided in mid-air with a cheerful "ker-ack" and then reeled about, me clutching my forehead, him clutching his nose. Or maybe he was clutching my forehead and I was clutching his nose. Precise memory fails me.

"Are you all right?" we said together.

"Yes!" I yelped, and hiccupped again.

And again.

And again.

"Gotta get that water," I gasped in the brief silence that followed, and cantered for the house.

At least I didn't fall over. That was some comfort.

Some. But not enough.

I crossed the fountainarium in four graceful bounds (boy,

143

was I ever getting the hang of those heels) and almost collided with Sara. Sándor bounced off the bottom step in
hot pursuit. Somebody must have spotted my encounter
with Pool God from the window. Upstairs I could hear
Noni screaming at them to get down and see if I was OK.
I was hiccupping so hard now I could barely speak. Sara
grabbed hold of me and I pointed wildly at my throat.

"She has ze hiccups again," Sándor interpreted,
helpfully. "She had zem before. She can vill zem avay."

Not this time, buddy.

In between eruptions I managed to croak out
"Water!" Sara shot behind the bar and grabbed a glass.

"No, no!" Sándor said. "Ice! She needs a shock!"

And while I was still registering this swift about turn
on the power of the will, he had also descended on the
bar, whipped the lid off the ice bucket, grabbed a handful of freezing cubes and shot them down the back of
my dress.

Aaaaargh!

It would have been bad enough if I'd been wearing a
looser fitting outfit. At least then they would have
dropped straight through and out onto the floor.
Instead they got as far as the middle of my back and
stuck. I felt as if I'd been stabbed with an icicle. Still
hiccupping wildly, I began to dance around, gasping
and clawing at my back. Sara appeared in front of me
with a glass of water.

"Drink this and hold your breath!" she said.

I shot back a mouthful and clamped down.

Hic!

Hic!

...

...

...

Hic!

I could feel my eyes bugging out of my head.

A shadow fell across me like the sun going into eclipse: Alec.

"She's got hiccups," said Sara. "I've just given her a drink of water. Now she needs to hold her breath."

Black dots were beginning to dance in front of my eyes. I let my breath out in a whoosh. Hiccups I could handle. Brain damage from oxygen starvation was another matter.

Hic!

"That won't do it," said Alec. "She has to get her head lower than her stomach and then drink it."

Sara seemed to buy this.

"Bend over," she said.

I bent over.

"Further."

Hic!

"I can't."

It was the heels.

"Not like that. Come here."

Next thing I knew Alec had grabbed hold of me by the waist and picked me up as if I was no heavier than a cocktail stick. He tipped me upside down and held me by the ankles while I scrabbled desperately at his legs.

"Give it to her now."

Sara appeared on her knees in front of me with the glass.

"Drink this!"

Gallons spilled up my nose.

"Now swallow," said Alec.

Gulp.

Maybe he'd put me down now.

"Give it a minute."

I shrieked and pummelled his shins.

The doors onto the garden slid open and a figure appeared.

"Excuse me," it said. "But there's something blocking your filter."

Pool God really knew how to pick his moments.

Even he seemed to realize he'd chosen a bad time. He goggled for second then said, "Oh, sorry" in a weird kind of voice.

We'd all stopped when he came in, Sara on her knees, Sándor bumbling about offering more ice, me swinging gently by my ankles against Alec's legs. Some kind of explanation seemed in order.

"She's got hiccups," said Alec and turned me right way up.

I would have preferred "We are all mad and enjoy tormenting this poor innocent creature in our spare time", but that would have been too much to hope for.

"Oh," said Pool God. If he'd sounded nervous before, he was obviously terrified now.

Back on my feet I yanked at my dress, which had ridden up my legs to an unseemly height. The thigh's the limit. And then, just to make my happiness complete, the ice cubes, which had now melted, decided this would be a good time to run down my back, down my legs and patter onto the floor in a little puddle round my feet. Oh great! No one needed to tell me what that looked like. Pool God shot me one horrified glance and backed out the door.

Sara was dabbing at me with a handful of cocktail napkins.

"I'm so sorry," she was saying. "Let's get you into

some dry clothes."

I looked down at her sadly.

"Don't bother," I said. "I'm going up to cut my wrists in the shower now. It wouldn't be worth the effort."

"Hey," said Alec. "Cured your hiccups!"

As if that was all that mattered.

I gave him my most evil look.

"Why don't you go out and see what the problem with the filter is?" I said, coldly. "And while you're at it, why don't you stick your head right under to get a good look at it? Oh, and don't bother coming up for air."

And I stalked out with as much dignity as I could muster, leaving nothing but that puddle and a trail of drips on the floor.

I could still hear Noni yelping as I went up the stairs. I flung the door open and stalked in.

"Darling! What happened? Are you all right?"

"No," I said, and my voice was surprisingly calm. "I'm not. I've been soaked to the skin, half frozen, and held upside down by the ankles in front of Pool God, who, in case you were wondering, is the guy currently trying to unblock your filter. I've had enough. Sorry, but there it is."

Noni gave a howl.

"No! You can't! You can't give up on me now."

"I'm not giving up," I said, which surprised even me. "I've had enough – for today. I'm going to my room to change into some human clothes now and I would be grateful if you could keep the Three Musketeers away from me for at least another hour. Especially Alec. If I see him again in the next few minutes I shall do something I shall regret. No, that's not true. I shan't regret it for a second, but you'll be looking for a new beauty consultant. I hate him. At the moment. Sara, I pity. Sándor, I love. But I need a break or I'll go mad."

And I walked out.

Silence.

Hey, Noni was actually lost for words.

A familiar pattering told me Madge was following me.

"You're too late," I said. "You missed all the fun. Why don't you go down and frighten Pool God? He probably thinks we've all got rabies."

The shower was so-o-o-o good. My own gear was even better. Bare feet was the best. I flopped onto the bed and stared up at the ceiling. I had a strange, exhilarating feeling of power. I had just mouthed off to Noni in a way that would have had any self-respecting disciplinarian bouncing me off the walls and all she had done was gawp. Maybe I was turning into her after all. That thought scared me.

I got up and put in a quick bout of pacing while I tried to reassess my position. OK, so I hadn't quit. Which I thought was pretty big of me. But I was getting nowhere fast. I could feel a howl of frustration welling up inside me. Maybe I should call Sadie. She was the person I usually howled at when the need arose. But then I would have to tell her what was bugging me and I wasn't too sure I could face it. Whatever her reaction, it was bound to be the one I would like least. It almost always was. But I needed to talk to someone: someone who wasn't three times my age, someone who didn't have anything to do with

Noni, someone, in effect, who wasn't here.

Jamie.

I don't why the thought popped into my head right then. I could see the piece of paper with his number on still lying on the table by the phone. I took half a step towards it, then hesitated. But I was still fizzing inside after my stand-off with Noni. If I couldn't pluck up the courage now, I never would. No time for second thoughts. I snatched up the paper and dialled.

His mother answered. At least I guessed that's who it was. Or maybe he had an unnatural taste for older women. Just my luck. Hey! I could pretend to be Noni. See how he liked that.

"Er… hi!" I said. "Is Jamie there?"

The older woman probably-his-mother didn't scream with horror, which was a good start. Instead she said, "Yes, he is, but we're about to go out. Who's calling?"

"Um … it's a friend he met the other week."

She didn't press me for further and better particulars, and I heard her turn away and shout "Jamie, there's a friend on the phone for you." There was the sound of lumbering and grunting (not her), and then a lumbering grunting voice said, "Hi!"

"Jamie?"

"Yeah?"

"It's Kat."

I squeezed my eyes tight and tried to keep my breathing slow and inaudible.

"Kat! Hey! Where are you?"

He sounded pleased! Less lumbery-grunty and distinctly human.

"I'm at my grandma's. In California."

"Oh wow!"

"My mom said you called by."

"Yeah, I hadn't seen you around and I wanted to say 'hi'. That friend of yours, I think it's Sadie, said you were in the States, but she didn't know when you'd be back. We finally made the move from Yorkshire, so I'm down here permanently now."

"That's great," I said, and I meant it. "But I'm not going to be back for at least a couple of weeks."

"Oh," he said, and I flatter myself he sounded disappointed.

There was still one issue I needed to clear up.

"Look," I said. "About the play…"

"Oh yeah," he said. "That was so funny. You were so funny."

OK, there was no need to rub it in.

"I know," I said. "I'm sorry. I wish you hadn't seen me like that. I'm not usually such a moron. Honest."

There, I'd said it.

"What do you mean?" he said. "I thought you were brilliant. What's-her-name, Sadie, told me about your grandma being a movie star. That acting thing obviously runs in the family."

I could hardly believe it: he didn't hate me; he didn't think I was a total jerk.

"Is that where you are now?" he was saying.

"Yes." I tried to sound enthusiastic. Things had been looking up. I just wish he hadn't felt the need to drag Noni into it. Or rather I wished what's-her-name-Sadie hadn't.

"That must be so neat," he said.

"It's OK," I said. "But there isn't all that much to do." (If you didn't count being coached for the world's worst personality transplant by a supporting team that wouldn't have looked out of place on Planet Zog.) "To be honest, I'd rather be back home in Oxford with you guys. Everyone here is so *old*."

There was the sound of muffled trumpeting in the background. Some distant mastodon-like creature calling to another. I heard Jamie turn away from the phone and trumpet something back.

"Listen," he said. "I've gotta go. But, it's so great you called. I wasn't sure you would. Let me know when you get back and maybe we could meet up."

May I live so long.

"Sure," I said. "We could do that."

The mastodon gave another quick blast.

"Gotta run," he said. "Be seeing you."

"Bye."

And he was gone.

Feeling strangely exhilarated, I fell back onto the bed and punched the air a few times. I'd done it. I'd called Jamie and he hadn't slammed the phone down in disgust. He'd even said he wanted to see me when I got back. Definitely a result.

Now what? Back to what passed for reality at Noni's fun house. As if on cue, I became aware of *Acting Against Character* prodding me in the shoulder. I rolled over and hauled it out from under the pillow. Maybe now would be a good time to finish it and see if dear old Sándor had any more insights for me. After all, there might be some things he'd forgotten since 1965. Unlikely, but worth a try. And what was that on the bedside table? Could it be? Oh yes! Some kindly soul had left me a bar of chocolate. A big one too. I reached for it and let it slide from the wrapper onto my stomach in a rustle of silver foil.

Let the healing commence!

\* \* \*

When I re-emerged (about an hour later), I was feeling ever so slightly nauseous (in an entirely good, chocolatey way), but at least the hiccups were a distant memory and I no longer wanted to scream and throw things.

They were all waiting for me in Noni's room. All of them except Wigan Man. Noni had sent him home. They all looked incredibly guilty. Ha! I didn't give them a chance to launch into their feeble apologies.

"OK," I said. "I'm ready to start again."

I felt rather than heard the collective sigh of relief. Sara was the first to speak.

"Do you want to choose a new outfit?" she asked, nervously.

"No," I said. "Not again. Not today. Please."

I looked at Sándor and waited for the objections to begin. But he merely clapped his hands.

"Excellent!" he said.

"Oh, and one other thing: I've decided what we're going to do tomorrow," I said.

It was worth it just to see the look on Noni's face.

LOCATION: PALM DESERT
TIME: DAY TWO OF THE GREAT KATRIONA SHAW MAKE-OVER DISASTER

The day did not begin well.

I woke to the sound of distant knocking and opened my eyes to see a large, familiar and totally unwelcome ginger mug grinning at me round the door. I groaned and rolled over.

"Hello, Ugly," said Alec.

"Ugly yourself," I mumbled through clenched sheets, then remembered my manners and pushed out a

152

reluctant: "Morning."

"Am I back in favour, or is some kind of penance still required?"

Penance? What kind of penance? Being Alec was a penance in itself.

He came round the bed. I kept my eyes tightly closed.

"Noni says you're planning on going out today."

I opened one eye. Sara had kindly put a bowl of fruit on the chest of drawers by the window. Alec was messing about juggling oranges.

"Stop it," I said. "You're making me dizzy."

He sat down by the bed and began twiddling a banana in his lap instead. I quickly closed my eye again.

"Tell me about it," he said.

I rolled onto my back trying to avoid the wag-wagging of the banana, but I could still see the horrible shadows it was casting on the ceiling.

"I need a test run," I said. "So I want to go to Palm Springs to see if I can pass as Noni there."

"OK," he said. "But how will you know if people recognize you or not?"

"I'm going to Rick's Place. He spotted Noni the minute she walked through the door. If I can pass as Noni with Rick, I'll feel I'm getting somewhere."

"Rick, eh? He has good shirts. I get all my shirts from him."

I risked a glance across at him. Today's offering was an unusually subdued affair in lime green with a discreet motif of orange pineapples. I couldn't believe Rick would let anything like that within a mile of his store. Alec seemed to expect some favourable comment.

"Rick's shirts are the best," I said, neutrally, and tried

153

to look as if I was admiring this particular eyesore. After all, I did need this man to do my face and hair, and I still hadn't forgotten those eyebrow tweezers. No need to upset him unnecessarily.

"Can I come?"

"No! Esteban's driving me, and I'm taking Sándor. If any more tag along it'll look like the circus has come to town." With him playing the part of Dumbo's mother. "Haven't you got things to do here?"

"Like what? If I give Noni any more deep facials, her nose will drop off."

"I don't know," I said. "Make something up. You should talk to my friend Sadie. She'd think of something. Like waxing her aura."

"I could massage her ego. Again."

"Whatever it takes."

"Anyway, I've been sent to tell you, if you want any snap, Sara is serving breakfast outside and Noni wants you to join her."

"Will Sándor be there or is he gnawing on a bone in the servant's quarters?"

He ignored this.

"Just get your idle backside out of bed," he said. "If you're visiting Rick, I'll be after spending that bit more time on you this morning."

He stood up and dropped the banana back in the dish.

"You can keep that," I said. "I don't fancy it now."

Noni was yapping on at me about what I should and shouldn't do on my next trip into civilization, while Sara piled my plate with pancakes and silently but expressively stood the jug of maple syrup next to my cappuccino. Sándor was chewing his way through something that looked like roadkill covered in yoghurt.

Probably some Hungarian specialty.

"You should take Madge," she was saying. As if having a rat-dog in tow was the answer to all my problems. Still, Noni always had been a woman who knew how to accessorize.

"Won't she get in the way? I'll have enough to think about without having to keep an eye on her. Remember last time. She and Junior nearly destroyed the store."

"Esteban will take care of her. And it will look odd if you don't. I go everywhere with Madge."

Hearing her name, the canine midget gem stuck her head out from under the table and grinned at me winsomely.

"OK," I said to her. "You can come, but you have to behave. Any nonsense and I'll get Esteban to shut you in the car."

She wagged her tail.

"In the boot?"

Waggle.

"I'm serious."

She gave a single excited bark.

"OK, just so you know."

Sándor swallowed his current mouthful of hedgehog surprise and said, "But ve must have a reason to go to zis shop. Ve cannot merely valk in and stand zere."

"I know, how about we buy something for you?"

"For me?"

"Yeah, why not. Another shirt or a pair of shorts or something."

Everyone looked at me.

"OK, maybe not shorts."

"And how do you propose to pay for them?" This was Noni.

"Can't you give me some money? I can let you have it back if we don't spend it."

"Money?" She made it sound as if I was proposing to haggle in livestock. "I don't use cash for that kind of purchase."

Well, excuse me!

"OK, so lend me your credit card."

She gave a little scream.

"Are you crazy?"

Obviously – I had to be mad to be doing this at all.

"Anyway, you can't copy my signature."

"You could teach me."

She writhed in her chair.

"Look," I said. "I promise I won't go mad and spend anything I shouldn't. Besides, what if someone recognizes me, or rather recognizes you, and wants an autograph?"

Good point.

"Oh, very well."

She made it sound as if she'd agreed to donate her body for research.

Sara helped me pick out my outfit for the day: a nifty little number in a colour Noni identified as "chartreuse," but which looked like green gak to me. Then it was over to Alec. I settled myself in what I had come to think of as the Chair of Unspeakable Torment.

"OK, time to work your magic," I said. "Mirror mirror in the loo, make me a woman of sixty-two."

He chuckled.

"Lovely lass, dressed all in green, I'll make you a vision fit for a queen."

I could only assume he was referring to Rick.

\* \* \*

We hit Palm Springs and parked at the mall. No skaters. I was disappointed. Even though I knew I wouldn't be able to join them, I'd still hoped to catch a welcome glimpse. But I already had my hands full with Sándor, who had been jigging about like a kid on a trip to the seaside since we left the house. I'd never seen anyone over the age of five look so excited.

Esteban held the car door open for me and I got out as gracefully as I could with Madge tucked under one arm. (Alec had given me a quick and surprisingly effective lesson in car-exiting before we left.) Sándor had already rolled out the other side and was zooming to and fro exclaiming "Zis is so great!" I didn't know anything about his home life, but I guessed he didn't get out much.

"Calm down," I said. "This is a small, overpriced hamlet in the middle of an arid wilderness, not the lost city of Atlantis."

"But zis is so great!"

Jig. Hop.

"Everyone will look at us if you carry on like that."

"But zat is vat ve vant, no?"

"No. Not everybody. Just Rick."

Hop. Jig.

"I won't buy you that shirt."

This seemed to calm him down. I clipped Madge's lead to her collar and put her down, and we headed for the entrance in a smart V-formation: me in front with Madge, Esteban and Sándor following at a respectful but attentive distance behind.

I could get used to this.

We swept through the mall, past the egg sculpture and out the other side. Rick's Place beckoned. I paused and breathed deeply. No hiccups. Yet.

"Well," I said. "Here goes."

Esteban stepped forward and pushed open the door. Madge, maybe scenting Junior, leapt forwards with a yip of excitement and I strode in with my head high, master of this particular universe (and that included the three-inch stack-heel espadrilles Sara had lashed me into under heavy protest that morning). OK, so Sándor, who was bobbing about beside me, didn't quite fit the image I was trying to put across, but I was Noni Waters and the presence of our in-house version of Mini-Me was the last thing to put a crimp in my style.

I angled myself towards the till, braced for squeals of either excitement or dismay, and saw a familiar face. But no familiar moustaches. The man standing behind the counter today was not Rick. Today's piece of prime desert manhood was ... you guessed it ... Pool God.

We goggled at each other for a minute.

"Miss Waters?"

I may only be fifteen – on my days off, that is – but I know barely suppressed terror and dismay when I hear them. This time I had to keep my cool. Not having Alec around to juggle me like a basket of fruit was a bonus.

"What are you doing here?" I said.

Calm, but firm.

I am in control. I *am* in control!

Then, feeling a surge of confidence – after all he had called me "Miss Waters", not "Kat" or "Impostor" or "Mad, drunken, incontinent old bag" – I added, "I thought you were supposed to be unblocking my filter."

"Oh," he said. "I help out here sometimes. As a favour to Rick. About the filter, I sorted that yesterday. I wanted to tell you, but…"

But? I could fill in the rest.

"Oh that," I said, trying to sound as if yesterday's performance was an everyday occurrence at the Waters residence. My mind was racing. What was I supposed to say? That I was trying out some new exercise routine? But that didn't explain the puddle. What I wanted to say was "You are the sexiest man I ever saw," but I reckoned now was neither the time nor place. Instead I gave a merry laugh. Yes, really. It was definitely a laugh and it was so merry it would have put your teeth on edge.

"I'm sorry I didn't get a chance to explain. What you must have thought!"

Another tinkling hahaha! My fillings began to ache in protest.

"I'm working on a new movie, and we were trying out one of the scenes. It's a comedy. Ha ha!" I thought of shoving in that bit about the sexual power of the older woman, but thought better of it on the same time and place grounds (see above). Instead I opted for: "It's a very physical part."

He seemed impressed.

"A new Noni Waters picture? Oh wow! When is it coming out?"

"Er … well, it's in the early stages right now," I improvised hastily. "And it's all rather hush-hush still." Time to go all winsome. "You won't tell anyone, will you?"

Any more of this and my teeth would be dropping right out of my head. He seemed to lap it up.

159

"Oh, I wouldn't dream of it, Miss Waters."

"It will be our little secret."

Oh, yuk! Gag gag gaggety gag! I couldn't take much more.

I could see him going all dewy-eyed.

"Where's Rick?" I asked, before he could go off oohing and aahing again.

"Rick just popped out for a minute with Junior. He'll be back soon. Can I help you?"

At least he didn't sound frightened any more, merely nervous. I could work with that.

"Yes! My granddaughter bought a couple of adorable shirts here and my friend, Mr Keczkes" – an airy wave in the direction of Sándor, who appeared to be dancing the Maypole with a display rack of ties – "would like something similar."

I was going to add, "If you have anything in his size" but realized that would have killed the project stone dead. Maybe the ties weren't such a bad idea.

"Yeah! Sure! Would you care to take a seat, Miss Waters?"

I hopped up on a helpfully placed stool with Madge in my lap, and he came round from behind the counter. Oh wow! I almost had to sit on my hands to stop myself reaching out and stroking his arms as he went past. He disentangled Sándor from the ties (literally) and released him onto the rails at the back of the shop. I looked across at Esteban, who was leaning against one of the mirrors on the wall, grinning quietly to himself. I raised my eyebrows (or what fragment of eyebrow Alec had left me), and he gave me a quick thumbs up.

So far so good.

I watched Pool God rummaging in the racks, trying

to find something vaguely suitable while Sándor plucked at the merchandise in a frenzy of delight. Then Esteban caught my eye and gave an imperceptible nod towards the door. Rick was heading in with Junior. I straightened my dress over my knees, ran my tongue over my teeth and took a firm grip on Madge's lead.

Time for the ultimate test.

Rick must have spotted me outside, because he hit the door at a run. He burst into the shop in a flurry of moustaches, Junior flying in behind him like a powder puff on the end of a lasso.

"Miss Waters!"

Good job I had that grip on Madge's lead or I would have been off that stool and face down in the carpet before you could say "Hello, sailor". Esteban swooped in skilfully on the dogs, leaving me to hold out both hands for a frenzy of knuckle snogging. Ew! His lips were moist and warm, and his moustaches tickled. Enough already! I withdrew the hands after what seemed like a decent interval, resisting the temptation to wipe them on my dress.

"You came back!" He looked around dramatically. "But where is your charming granddaughter?"

If you only knew, Mister.

"She's out with friends. Skateboarding."

She wished.

"She loved the shirts."

"She did?"

"I have a visitor and he admired them so much I brought him here today."

Rick swivelled and surveyed the store. No Sándor. Only Pool God, Esteban and the two dogs, who had picked up their antics where they had been forced to leave off last time and were careering round like a pair of animated ear muffs. Then the curtain over one of the changing rooms was pulled back and Sándor emerged. Rick put his hand over his heart and shrieked. Esteban made a strange, strangled noise behind me, and even I, who was used to him by now, rocked back on the stool.

He was wearing a shirt that would have put even Alec's brightest, boldest effort to shame. It was yellow, it was purple, it was green. Palm trees, guitars, surfboards, exotic looking fruit all jostled for position against a background that could have been meant to resemble a sunset, but in reality looked like one large bruise. And it was huge. It hung virtually to his knees, the sleeves wafting baggily around pathetically skinny elbows. The Sándor Keczkes we knew and loved, that strange, gnarled, but adorable Sándor Keczkes was no more. This Sándor Keczkes was an eyesore. If he was a fashion victim, that shirt should have been charged with grievous bodily harm.

He stood grinning at us like some psychedelic fireplug, obviously taking our silence for admiration.

"Zis," he said in tones of triumph and delight, "I like."

Rick looked at Pool God. Pool God looked helpless. I stared at Sándor.

"Sándor," I said. "It's hideous. Take it off."

"But I like it."

"You can't," I said. "No one could."

"On the right person…" Rick began.

"There is no right person for that," I said.

Sándor had begun a sideways approach to the mirror. I didn't want to see him hurt.

"Sándor, darling, I really don't think…"

162

He was looking at himself. Oh well, maybe it was best for him to find out the hard way.

"I like it!"

"Wouldn't you like a nice tie instead?"

"No, I like zis."

He was becoming petulant.

Rick leaned over and whispered in my ear, "Miss Waters, for you I'll knock twenty per cent off. I've been trying to get rid of that one for months."

I looked him in the eye.

"Make it twenty-five and we'll take it."

"It's yours."

How about that? I snapped open my bag and produced the magic card with the same casual flourish I'd seen Noni use before. He almost caught it before it hit the counter.

"May I wrap the shirt for you, sir?"

Absolutely you may, and set fire to the bundle when you're done, I thought.

"Zank you, no, I shall keep it on."

I suppressed a groan. I wondered how fast I could walk in these espadrilles to make it look like we weren't actually together. Now I was glad the skater guys weren't there. Even dressed as Noni the humiliation would be intense.

A credit slip appeared in front of me with a huge X next to the line marked "signature" and I dashed off a businesslike version of the Waters autograph. I swear I saw Rick stroke it as he tucked it into the cash register, but maybe it was because he was so glad to be rid of that shirt.

"We must be going," I said, as graciously as possible. No point pushing my luck. "Esteban, if you could catch Madge for me."

Rick bounded to open the door.

"Miss Waters, it has been such a pleasure."

A laugh a minute. I was aware of Sándor hovering behind me like some luminous alien virus.

Rick began twirling his moustaches.

"Miss Waters, I wonder if I might ask you a tremendous favour?"

Ask away, buddy. Two more days and I was off the hook, anyway.

"I run a little society here in Palm Springs. It's just me and a few like-minded friends who are all huge fans of yours, and every fall we hold a competition where we dress up as characters from your movies."

I looked at him, appalled. Whatever happened to stamp collecting? Get a life!

"And I wondered if, this year, you would do us the tremendous honour of judging our annual Best Miss Noni Waters contest?"

Oh brother! Grown men dressing up as my grandmother? Grown men with moustaches dressing up as my grandmother? I mean, puh-leez! I was about to trot out a brisk "I don't really think so," when something stopped me. Why not? Who was I to put the "No" in Noni? It would do her good. She needed to get out and meet more people. Even strange and delusional ones like Rick and his merry band. I smiled my most charming smile.

"Why, I'd be delighted," I said. "Let me know nearer the time."

Ah revenge, sweet revenge! I was almost sorry I wouldn't be there to watch the show.

I turned back for a last fond glimpse of Pool God. Poor, glorious Pool God: a rose among some seriously demented thorns.

"Do come back and check on that filter soon," I said, and I hoped it sounded tempting.

I let Rick have another go at my hands as I left. He seemed moister than ever, but I think it was because he was crying with joy.

As the door closed behind me I let out a long, deep sigh of relief. I had done it! I had looked like Noni. I had acted like Noni. I had *been* Noni. Half of me was elated. The other half was appalled. I couldn't recall a single thing I had said in there that would ever have come naturally to the lips of Katriona Shaw. It was all pure Noni. I shuddered. Sándor and his Amazing Technicolour Eyesore appeared on the sidewalk at my elbow (literally). I shuddered again and took off at a brisk clip, trying to put as much distance between us as possible. If the green of my dress was unforgiving, that shirt was unforgivable. We clashed like a pair of cymbals. As I burst out of the doors at the far end of the mall and turned into the home stretch I was several lengths ahead and moving well.

The skaters were there.

That brought me up sharp. I was torn between wanting to dawdle and watch them, and wanting to stay well ahead of Sándor, the walking migraine. Lucas was there and I could see him looking across at me. Surely he hadn't recognized me? Then I remembered that the first time I'd seen him I was with Noni, who'd hauled me away as if I'd been showing an unseemly interest in a gang of sore-infested beggars. Time to build some bridges. OK, so I hadn't gone mad with the card. I'd even saved Noni some money (in exchange for severe visual pain). But there were other ways to exploit her credit. Rick's little beauty contest had been one. Now I

165

spotted the opportunity for another. I didn't want Noni's money, but, let's face it, the woman definitely owed me.

I did a quick mental tweak to put myself back into full Noni mode and stepped out across the car park towards them. Lucas saw me coming and whizzed to a halt. I waved to him.

"Young man!"

Good, eh?

He ambled over, looking wary.

"Yes, ma'am?"

I loved it!

"You were skateboarding here with my granddaughter the other day."

"Yes, ma'am."

Still wary. Who could blame him? He'd seen the real Noni in guard dog mode.

"I just wanted to tell you she had a wonderful time. It was kind of you."

He brightened up.

"Gee, no problem. She was cool."

He thought I was cool! Resisting the sudden urge to hop from one foot to the other waving my fists in the air and shouting "Yes!" I smiled.

"I hope she can meet up with you again sometime."

Now he became animated.

"Sure, it's vacation and we're here most days. We'll be here tomorrow."

Schneider day.

"We have other plans tomorrow, I'm afraid. But maybe the day after...?"

May I live so long.

He grinned.

"Yeah! That would be great. We'll be here."

166

Yes!

"I'm sure she'll be able to come then."

"Cool! Oh and" – he looked shy – "I loved her accent. It's just like yours."

???

Better put in some voice work this evening.

Suddenly his head snapped up and his eyes widened. I looked round.

Sándor had emerged from the mall.

"Excuse me," I said. "I have to go."

He barely heard me.

"Look at that shirt!" he was saying. "Awesome, dude!"

LOCATION: PALM DESERT, THE SICK ROOM
TIME: AFTERNOON

Noni was falling over herself (her specialist manoeuvre) to hear how the outing had gone. After she'd recovered from the sight of Sándor ("How much did you pay for that shirt?") she wanted to know every last detail. I gave as full an account as I deemed wise, omitting the bit about her election to the Best Miss Noni Waters judging panel, and the planned meeting with the skaters at the mall. She was pleased. Sándor, who was sitting in the corner, pulsing with evil light, kept chipping in with supportive comments; and Esteban added his twopence worth to say I'd looked the part and stayed in character throughout. Even Madge gave me a vote of confidence by staying in my lap and ignoring Noni's calls of "Come to Mommy, baby girl."

"That's wonderful!" Noni said. "Well done, darling!"

I had to say, I was feeling pretty pleased with myself.

167

Not that I thought the Sam Schneider thing was going to be a pushover, but at least I felt a whole lot better than I had before.

"Of course," she went on, "what you have to remember is that people like Rick only really know me from my movies. It's not the same as getting to know someone in person. With Sam it will be different. He and I have known each other and worked closely together for over forty years."

What was that I just said about feeling better? Well, cancel it.

Oh well, I suppose now was as good a time as any to put in a good, long, sleepless night. And I couldn't wait to get out of these plastic talons and indulge in some serious nail-biting. Come the morning I confidently expected to have reduced my fingers to bleeding stumps. It seemed a reasonable price to pay.

*When I put Noni's clothes on, things change. I change. I can't help it. There's something about altering your appearance that makes you feel differently about who you are. I think it's all tied up with how you know other people see you and how you see yourself. Take Noni. Remember the conversation we had about that time when she was little? I said I understood what she meant and I did. In a way. But in the way that was me imagining myself thinking the same thing. I felt I knew her a little better after that, but couldn't see her any differently. And that's kind of scary. The outside is so important. I'm not saying it's right to judge people by appearances, but there are different ways of judging people. It's not OK to decide someone is good or bad because of the way they look. And it's not OK to treat people badly because of the way they look. But we can't help seeing the way someone is and making certain assumptions. When Alec and Sara have finished and I'm standing there in front of the mirror I don't see me any more. I see Noni. I can't help it. And from there it's not such a big step to being her. But I'm being her the way I see her. I don't know how Sam Schneider sees her. I can't know that. And it scares me. I want to do my best for her. I really do. But I don't know if the Noni I can be tomorrow will be Sam Schneider's Noni. I would ask her who that is, but I know she couldn't tell me. So tomorrow when Sam Schneider comes, I'll be Noni. But it'll be Kat's Noni. Maybe we both see enough of the same things in her to make it all right. I hope so. It's the best I can do. The best Noni I can be.*

*I hope he likes her.*

LOCATION: PALM DESERT
TIME: D-DAY, THE GREAT KATRIONA SHAW MAKE-OVER
DISASTER DAY

I did sleep. A bit. But today was the first day since I'd arrived that I didn't have to be woken up for breakfast. At seven I went down and swam. The morning was new and fresh and beautiful. Everything I wasn't. I swam up and down on my back, looking up hopefully at the pink and blue sky and wishing I was anywhere but here. If ever there was a time to be abducted by aliens, this was it. Let them do their worst. It could hardly beat the ordeal that lay ahead of me.

A gloomy half hour passed. I'd been in the water long enough. No point going all pruniferous and upsetting Alec. I stood up and looked at my hands. He'd have his work cut out this morning trying to find enough original material to stick those false nails onto as it was. I hauled myself out and dribbled my way inside for a hot shower before it was time to face my public.

Breakfast was early. Il Schneiderissimo was expected at 10.30. All the troops had reported in. I was allowed to eat before getting ready, on the grounds that otherwise I might spill something on my dress. Thanks for the vote of confidence, Noni. I chewed my way through Sara's spectacular offerings, hardly noticing what I was eating. It was sacrilege, but I was too caught up in my own dread thoughts to care. Noni was yipping at her about lunch.

"Nothing that's difficult to eat. After the salad – Katriona, you do eat goat's cheese, don't you, darling? – salmon. No sauce. Plain grilled. Do we have asparagus? Good. No dessert. Fruit."

No dessert? Even Sara looked surprised.

"I made a chocolate hazelnut cake. No flour. It's good."

"I don't think so."

"Hey!" I said. "I do. I want it."

Noni looked at me severely.

"It will look odd if you eat that. I wouldn't."

"People change."

"People get fat."

"I don't."

She sighed.

"Oh, very well, but only one slice."

Yes! One bright light on an otherwise gloomy horizon. Something to make up for the goat's cheese.

After Sara's lecture on appropriate foodstuffs, it was my turn to be briefed.

"Remember all the things I've told you. Again –

what does Sam like?"

We'd been through this a hundred times.

"He only drinks coffee. No tea. He's allergic to avocado. He likes flying and has two planes of his own: one Cessna, one Learjet. If he asks, I'm not to agree to go up with him, as the one time you did, you were sick everywhere."

"Not quite everywhere," muttered Noni.

"And he's on the board of the Opera and the Philharmonic. But you say he's tone deaf. So? I'm hardly going to ask him to sing. He's a Capricorn and his favourite colour is pink."

"What?"

"I made that last bit up."

"Please don't goof around, Katriona. This is serious. Now: dislikes."

Me, goof around? What did she think she'd been doing when she fell off my skateboard?

"OK, dislikes: cats, spiders, his third wife, science fiction, Mexican food, rock music" – (The man was obviously a total wuss.) – "oh, and Pisceans and the colour blue."

"Katriona!"

"Sorry."

"Now, if you've had quite sufficient, I'll ask Sara to clear the dishes and you can get ready."

I knew things were serious because even Alec was being nice to me. He tut-tutted over the nails, but didn't bawl me out like he would have done normally. Sara, Noni and I had already picked out my outfit. Noni wanted a backless number in shocking pink. I kicked like a mule at that one. I wasn't about to go out and face anyone, let alone Sam Schneider, looking like a half-eaten popsicle. I requested something more substantial in black, but Noni objected that I wasn't going to a funeral. I said I might as well be, which earned me a nasty look. Sara, the one voice of sanity, had a rummage and came up with a racy little number in peacock blue silk. That I could bear. Even Noni approved. It came with the obligatory scarf, matching sling backs with, oh wow, only two-and-a-half inch heels, and after a bit of a confabulation, we settled on a broad-brimmed hat in white. Sara said it would help shade my face. Fine. It couldn't be too big for me. Then, if things went completely pear-shaped, I could whip it off, climb inside and pull the brim down over my head.

Thirty minutes later I was ready. I stood in front of the mirror with that sinking feeling, looking at the Noni of the day. She looked good. Let's face it, she looked sensational. What a shame she felt like a fifteen-year-old know-nothing about to go into the world's toughest exam knowing she hadn't done enough revision.

It was 10.15.

I went through to Noni. Sándor was with her.

"Darling," she said, and held out her hands. I went over to be kissed. She wouldn't let me go. I sat down on the bed and let her put her arms round me. She smelled of faded perfume and coffee. She smelled of Noni. I blinked hard, trying not to let any tears sneak out and ruin my mascara. I felt her sniff in my shoulder. When she let go of me there was a small damp patch on the sleeve of the dress. I hoped it would dry.

"I'll do my best," I said. "I promise."

"I know you will, darling."

Sniff.

She fumbled around for a handkerchief.

Sándor looked serious.

172

"You vill concentrate and remember everyzink I have told to you. But you must relax and let your instincts carry you zrough. Ve have trained zem to respond to your vill, as you know."

Relax? Ooh, yes, that was likely. And right now my instincts were telling me to leap through the window, shin down the flowering trellis and head for the hills.

"Of course, Sándor," I said meekly.

I could already hear a car outside.

"He's here! Quick, down you go. You're supposed to be in the study when he comes in. Madge! Where's Madge?"

"Sara's already taken her downstairs."

"Good luck, darling. Break a leg!"

You mean like you nearly did?

Sándor gave me a little bow.

"Even if he realizes you are not Noni, he vill love you," he added gravely, which was the nicest thing anyone could have said. Then he stood up on his wee tippy toes and kissed me too, which was even nicer.

Doors slammed outside.

"Quick!" cried Noni. "Oh, and – one more thing, darling."

I paused in the door. Now what? My brain was already going into overdrive with all the instructions.

"Do be kind to Sam. Please. He's always had a soft spot for me, you know."

As I ker-lunked my way downstairs to the study, I thought about that one. What did she mean? But I could guess. Oh brother. Sándor had suggested that I should try and keep a reasonable distance between me and Sam Schneider at all times, to stop him getting too close a look. I had wondered what a reasonable distance might be. Now I thought I knew. About six light years suddenly seemed about right.

The doorbell rang. I grabbed a book and flipped it open. It was upside down. Who cared?

Sara's head appeared round the door.

"Are you ready?"

I nodded dumbly.

"Here's Madge."

I picked her up. She wriggled and licked my sunglasses. At least there was one living soul in the building who didn't really care who I was.

I heard Sara cross the hallway and open the door.

Voices.

I looked at Madge.

"Toto," I said. "I don't think we're in Kansas any more."

I had seen enough photos of Sam Schneider to recognize the man standing in the atrium. What I hadn't expected was that he would be quite so old, or quite so bald, or quite so tanned, or quite so much larger than life. OK, so he looked like he'd been in movies since before they invented sound, but energy cackled off him. Geriatric but feisty, if you can imagine that.

"Noni Waters!" he yelled and swooped down on me.

"Sam!" I managed to get out before he had grabbed me and given me, if not exactly the snogging of my life, a quick all-over squeeze and several good hard wet ones. Thank God for the scarf.

Then he held me away from him and looked me up and down. I met his gaze square on and tried to radiate Noni-ness. He took so long I began to think my smile was about to meet round the back of my head and tie itself in a knot. I knew he was supposed to be short-sighted, but this was ridiculous. Then I had a nasty thought. Oh no! Maybe he wasn't so myopic after all.

"Noni, you look sensational! You don't look a day over twenty!"

Inward sigh of relief.

Oh, Schneider, if you but knew...

"Come through!" I chirruped. "Sara will get us something to drink. Coffee? Something cold? I know you won't want tea."

I waved him towards the fountainarium. At this time of day it was reasonably shady. Good cover.

"Something cold sounds good. Iced coffee?"

"Absolutely, darling."

I gave Sara the nod and she beetled off to fill our order.

"This is Madge," I said, offering her like a tray of cocktail snacks to be fondled. Rather her than me.

"Cute," he said, and tried to pat her head.

She growled.

Uh-oh.

"Silly girl," I said and laughed, not especially hysterically. This I needed. A canine protector just when everyone was supposed to be making nice.

"Where would you like us to sit?" I said, thinking opposite corners would be a good idea.

"How about you and me get cosy on the sofa?"

And before I could come up with a better suggestion like "How about you on the sofa and me somewhere like Arizona," he'd thrown himself onto it in a jangle of gold chains (did I mention the jewellery? – through the gaping neck of his shirt, his chest looked like a Saxon grave hoard) and was patting the cushions next to him.

Gulp.

I sauntered over and sat down. Near him. Near, but not close. And to keep it that way I plopped Madge down between us. Time for that little madam to earn her keep.

"You remember the house?" I said. It was a strategy Sándor had come up with: "If you take control of the conversation you vill be able to direct much of vat is said."

Noni had helped out with some possible topics and told me what she thought he was likely to say. The house seemed a safe kicking-off point.

"Oh yes," he said. "I remember this house."

There was something about the way he said it I didn't quite like. On top of which I thought I detected what was usually known in polite circles as a leer. And I wasn't talking about his private jet.

Quick. Time to try something else. Noni had told me to make small talk first, but Sam's reaction had scared me off. Small talk, big ideas. I decided to kick right into business.

"So," I said, and clasped my hands in my lap. (This was partly to stop myself from reaching out and buttoning up that shirt. Yeesh! For a guy who was bald as an egg, he sure had a lot of body hair. I thought Alec was bad; the last time I saw anything as ginger and hairy as him it was advertising kitty kibbles. But Sam Schneider was unbelievable. It was everywhere: his arms, even the backs of his hands! And, yes, quick double check, enough growing out his ears to stuff several pillows and still have sufficient left over to keep a family of hamsters in comfort for the whole of the winter.)

I had to concentrate.

"The movie. This is so exciting. Tell me about it."

If he'd been expecting more of a build up, it didn't

176

show. He cracked his knuckles – hairy knuckles! – and said, "Absolutely, Noni. Of course, you read the script."

Of course I had.

"And you know what your part is essentially about?"

I certainly did!

He looked at me expectantly.

I wasn't saying it. No way.

"The sexual power of the older woman."

Surprise!

"And, of course, as soon as that was pitched to me, I said 'Noni Waters. It has to be Noni Waters.'"

I tried to look gratified.

"Don't look like that," he said.

OK, maybe it had come out looking more like horrified.

"It's true. And what did they say? I'll tell you what they said. They said, 'But Noni Waters hasn't made a picture in years. She's retired.' And d'you know what I said to them?"

I didn't, but I was sure he was about to tell me.

"I said, 'I don't care. She's the one.'"

"That was very kind of you, Sam."

He clearly expected something bigger. I did my best.

"I mean, I was overwhelmed. Like you say. It's been so long. And I haven't thought of myself ... er ... that way for ... oh..."

I made vague fanning gestures in the air.

"Are you crazy?"

Yes.

"You always were the hottest thing on screen."

I blushed a becoming pink.

He winked.

"And off."

The pink deepened to an unlovely red.

He shifted towards me and reached out a hand. I watched in horrified fascination. Don't recoil and scream! Do not recoil and scream!

Madge growled again.

The hand withdrew.

"That's quite a little dog you got there," he said resentfully.

"Isn't she just too adorable?" I said and tickled her ears.

Sam didn't look like he thought so.

Sara came in with the drinks.

"Any chance we eat?" said Sam. "I hope you don't mind my asking, but I had breakfast in LA at six and I'm getting hungry."

Fine by me. Food was always good. And it would keep Hairy Hands occupied. I looked at Sara.

"I'll serve lunch outside," she said.

Outside was good. More places to run and hide. And if he got too carried away, I could always shove him in the pool.

We strolled out and Sara took the drinks over to the table under the umbrella. Good. Separate chairs. None of this sofa-sidling nonsense.

The move seemed to have calmed him down. We sipped our coffees and chatted about the film business. No trick questions yet.

"You really do look amazing," he said. "Who's your beautician? Whoever it is, is a genius."

"You know Monsieur Alexander?"

"What? That baboon?"

Which was good coming from him.

He laughed. I scowled. And not just with my ears.

178

"He's wonderful," I said, coldly. "He really understands my face."

"He must do. Like I said, you don't look a day over twenty. So why all the headgear? Are you afraid to let me see you?"

From your lips to God's ears!

I tried a careless laugh.

"Oh, you know, it's the sun. Death to skin."

That should strike a chord. Noni had told me his second wife, a dedicated sun worshipper, had died of skin cancer. It certainly shut him up for a moment.

"One can't be too careful."

"At least I can see your legs. You always had terrific legs."

I slammed my knees tight together under the table.

Sara appeared with a trolley. Just in time. Cutlery clattered.

"Would you care for some wine, sir?"

We'd prepared this one.

Sam Schneider rubbed his hands.

"A glass of white would be terrific. Noni?"

I smiled bravely and shook my head.

"Not for me, thank you. I hardly touch alcohol at all nowadays."

"You don't?"

Does the Pope wear a dress?

The salad appeared. Goats' cheese. Hmmm. Cheese I like. But cheese that has the texture of play-dough and tastes of sweat? I don't think so. But as today was dedicated to "let's pretend", I reckoned I could force it down.

Sam got his wine. I got mineral water. Low on taste, but high on hurlability: a highly effective form of defence in a tight spot.

179

I filled my glass.

Eyes down. Eat. Munch crunch. Munchety crunch.

Quite the salad.

Sam was yakking on between mouthfuls – no, make that during mouthfuls (yuk!) – about his movies and my movies. Yada yada yada. I made suitable noises and kept eating. The salad was full of those large curly, springy leaves that are kind of difficult to subdue. I thought Noni had said to keep it easy. I hoped Sara had washed it properly. It looked like there could be an army of creepy-crawlies in there and you wouldn't notice until you bit into one. Or it bit into you.

It was unfortunate that this was the moment I felt something tickling my leg.

I glanced down. Then up. Then down again.

Help!

The biggest creepy-crawly I'd ever seen was making its way slowly but determinedly up my thigh. It was huge, it was covered in hair. It had more legs than a rugby team.

Tarantula!

And Sam Schneider hated spiders!

I screamed and stuck my fork right in the middle of its back.

All hell broke loose.

I flew backwards off my chair, clutching my napkin to my chest and gibbering. Madge woke up from where she'd been dozing on her favourite lounger and began barking hysterically. But if there'd been a prize for "Most Dramatic Reaction", Sam Schneider would have won hands down. He took off from a seated position and flew straight up into the air, catching his knees on the underside of the table and sending the whole thing over with an ear-splitting smash of plates, glasses and clattering cutlery. I was dimly aware of a single spoon somersaulting away across the tiles and falling with a distant *splosh* into the pool.

I came back to earth, followed a good two seconds later by Sam.

We stared at each other.

Somewhere above us I heard a window slam open.

"You stuck your fork in my hand," he said in a voice shaking with disbelief. "You stuck your frigging fork in the back of my hand."

Sara came out of the house at a run.

His hand?

He was sucking it now. I stared.

Yup. There it was. Huge, hairy and ugly as sin. The last time I'd seen anything so vile had been in a TV documentary on the insect life of the Amazon rain forest.

And it had been crawling up my leg!

He glared at me.

I glared back.

"Of course I stuck my fork in your hand," I shouted. "What did you expect me to do?"

Don't allow him to take control of the conversation, Sándor had said.

Be kind to him – that was Noni.

Nobody had said anything about having to fight him off with the cutlery.

Sara was crouched over the mess.

"What happened?" she said.

I didn't take my eyes off Sam.

"Mr Schneider thought he saw a spider," I said, loud enough for the earwiggers at the upstairs window to hear.

What the hell. I'd totally blown it now anyway.

"He doesn't like spiders."

Sara looked bewildered.

"It's OK," I said. "But he may need a Band-aid for his hand."

"It bit him?"

Now she looked horrified.

"Kind of. Not exactly. But..."

Sam Schneider removed his hand from his mouth and looked at it. I looked at it. Sara got up and looked at it.

There was a neat line of four prong marks square in the middle of all those hairs. I hadn't even broken the skin. Damn!

"That was one hell of a spider," he said. Then he grinned. "And, Noni, you're one hell of a girl."

I hoped Sara couldn't hear that; she was busy trying to catch Madge, who was in danger of cutting her paws on the broken glass.

"If that was the starter what's the entrée?"

"Grilled salmon," I said.

"Sounds good. Only question is, where do we eat now?"

Esteban appeared with broom as if by magic and Sara set us up at another, smaller table by the pool.

"Terrific," said Sam. For some reason the whole incident seemed to have put him in an exceptionally good mood. "Then if you decide on a flambé and set fire to my legs, I can jump straight in the water. You always did think of everything, Noni."

We got through the rest of the meal without any further disasters. And Sam kept his hands to himself. After coffee and a superb chocolate hazelnut cake he wiped his mouth with a sigh of satisfaction, crossed his hands on his stomach and grinned at me wolfishly.

182

"How about you show me the garden?" he said. "And then I can tell you some more about the picture."

The garden? This hadn't been part of the homework. I didn't know what anything was. Maybe I could make it up. Maybe he wouldn't ask.

I got up, trying to look like this was my idea of heaven.

"The garden. Oh yes! That!"

"You always did love plants, didn't you?"

I did?

"Little Miss Green Thumbs we used to call you. Remember?"

Little Miss What? He smiled, looking even more wolf-like than ever. How about Little Red Riding Hood? This may be Grandmother's house, but you can't trust everything you see in a white straw bonnet, peacock silk cocktail gown and matching sling-backs.

"Shall we?"

He took my hand and slipped it through his arm.

Oh gross! I could feel all that hair tickling the inside of my elbow. I looked round for Madge. She'd fallen asleep on the lounger again. Useless hound. Esteban had finished clearing up and gone off to dispose of the remains. I was alone. I only wished I'd had enough foresight to shove a couple of mousetraps in the tops of my stockings, but I guess it would have spoiled the line of my dress.

Actually, he behaved quite well. We ambled about, pointing out this and that. Which meant him pointing and me wondering "what's that?" Then he began to reminisce. Uh-oh, danger. What if he came up with something I didn't know about? Probably something Noni had been too embarrassed to tell me.

Too late.

"Do you remember that time I signed Louise Schell for that Warner Brothers picture about the Polish nun, and you were so mad you set fire to my car?"

I'd done what? Or rather, Noni had done what? She *was* mad.

"Oh, that!" I said, and tried a careless laugh.

"And that premiere for *Ocean's Dream*? Where you tripped over Hannibal Crosby's guide dog and nearly fell on your butt?"

Er, no, I couldn't say that I did.

I felt his hand descend on my bottom. Fuzz tickled the side of my head.

"And what a delicious little butt it was, and still is," his voice purred in my ear.

Squeeze.

Why had I ever let go of that fork?

Squeeze squeeze squeezy squeeze.

I closed my eyes.

Help me, somebody! Anybody.

"What the hell is that?"

???

The pressure relaxed. I opened my eyes again. I couldn't see anything unusual.

"You have a skateboard?"

My skateboard! I'd forgotten all about it. Esteban must have left it there that night we had to take Noni to the clinic.

"Oh, yes," I said, completely forgetting who I was supposed to be. "Isn't it great?"

Too late I realized my mistake.

"I mean, it belongs to my granddaughter. She's not here right now. She's ... er ... in Hawaii with a friend."

At least he'd let go of my bum.

184

"She painted it herself. You want to see?"

I bounded quickly away. No more hands. No more grabby grabby. I picked it up. At least I now had a get-away vehicle. I held it up between us like a shield.

"Hell," he said. "I never thought I'd see you with one of those. You'll be telling me you can skateboard yourself next. Now that would be something for the movie."

My professional pride was stung. The bum thing had thrown me. I was losing my sense of judgement.

"Well, of course I can," I said. "I'm not just a pretty face, you know."

"Show me."

He had to be kidding.

"Go on. This I have to see."

"OK," I said and, tucking it under my arm, I marched back to the pool.

I dropped the board on the tiles and put one foot onto it. Alarm bells were ringing in my head: You're supposed to be sixty-two! *Sixty-two!* And then, more loudly. Not in heels! NOT IN HEELS!

Too late. It was a matter of pride now.

I pushed off and trundled the length of the pool. Sam was watching, clearly fascinated. Encouraged, I tried a few simple manoeuvres. So far so good. He had begun to applaud. I was gaining in confidence. How about that trick Lucas had shown me? OK, so I hadn't quite mastered it, but it was worth a try. I scooted to the far end of the pool to get a run up and set off back towards him so he could get the full effect. I reckoned about halfway would give me enough room. I judged the spot and went for it: jump, twist, land, swivel, kick and – oops!

The board flew out from under me and took off at

speed. As I landed heavily on one foot I could see Sam gazing at it, rooted to the spot as it soared through the air towards him.

No-o-o-o!

Everything went into slow motion. I could feel my mouth opening to shout a warning, but it was too late. The sharp end caught him right in the serious part of the trousers and he went down without a sound.

Then Madge woke up, took one look at him, decided enough was enough, hurled herself forward and sank her teeth into his leg.

This time he really did need that Band-aid.

We carried him inside, moaning softly, and laid him on the sofa. Sara ran to get the first aid box for the bite on his ankle, Esteban went behind the bar to pour a glass of brandy, and I knelt on the floor holding his hand and babbling apologies while he lay there doing the kind of whole-body writhe you don't often get to see in real life. Madge, the people's champion, had been banished to the laundry room. Upstairs was ominously silent, as if the house was holding its breath. The way little kids do in the first few seconds after they've fallen down and haven't quite figured out how bad the damage is. I expected the screaming would kick in later. Probably the second Sam Schneider was out of earshot.

After about five minutes, he opened his eyes long enough to spot the brandy, which I was now holding, and I saw his fingers twitch towards it. We propped him up on a pillow, and I helped him take a couple of sips. Then he closed his eyes again and we had another few minutes' respectful silence. At last his lips moved, in a non-writhy way.

"Noni."

"Sam?"

"You nearly killed me."

I stroked his hand. The hair actually had a pile to it like a carpet. Stroke it this way and it caught the light just so. Stroke it the other way, the colour went darker. Huh!

"I know. I'm sorry!"

Somehow "sorry" seemed rather a pale expression to make up for the indignity, never mind the agony, I'd caused him.

"It was an accident, Sam."

Like that was going to make him feel any better.

He took some more brandy.

It seemed to help.

He blinked and shook his head. I noticed his eyes had little red rims to them, but at least they'd stopped watering like the fountain trickling away centre-stage behind us.

"You are unbelievable," he croaked after a few more seconds staring into the brandy glass. "Noni Waters on a skateboard?"

"I'm sorry."

Maybe if I said it often enough, it would work.

He shook his head again.

"No," he said. "It was terrific. At first."

So, I guessed he wouldn't be writing that particular stunt extravaganza into the movie for Noni to deal with. But then he'd probably written her out of the movie full stop. If he really thought he was jinxed, the last thing he was going to do was sign up to work with a woman who'd tried to kill him not once, but twice within less than an hour of letting him through the front door. This didn't seem like a good time to ask.

"You know," he said. "When I was lying there on

187

the ground, I had the most bizarre experience, like a vision. I must have been hallucinating with the pain. Up on the roof – I thought I saw that old fraud Sándor Keczkes wearing the ugliest goddam shirt you ever saw."

After another twenty minutes and several more brandies he made it onto his feet and stood, rocking gently as if he was surprised he could stand at all.

"Noni," he said. "I gotta go."

"You do?"

"I do. Really. I think that's best."

I bit my lip. I couldn't believe I had messed up this badly.

"Sam…" I said. "I wish…"

He reached out cautiously and patted my arm.

"I'll be OK."

"About the movie?"

I had to ask.

He managed a wry smile.

"I'll call you," he said.

I knew what *that* meant. I tried not to hang my head.

"You do that," I said. "Please."

This time I took his arm without being asked and helped him as he hobbled to the front door and out to where his car was waiting. His driver hurried forward when he saw the state he was in, but Sam waved him away with a gruff, "I'm fine."

"Sam, it was so good to see you. I'm sorry…"

He squeezed my hand. OK, the hand I could cope with.

"You know something?" he said.

I knew I was the world's biggest fraud. And a loser.

"It never would have worked out with you and me."

?

"It takes a tough guy to handle you, Waters."

Yeah, like a guy with iron underpants.

"I always thought I was tough, but you run rings round me. I never understood why you married those other guys. They weren't men enough for you. You shoulda stuck with that guy I met that time in New York. I forget his name. Zebedee. No, that wasn't it. Zachary! – Zachary Waters. He was the only one who had you straight. And then you went and dumped him for that dumb ass, Joely Swinburne. Mistake, Waters."

He actually chuckled.

"Hey, stuff happens. Anyway, it was terrific to see you too. Even if I barely got out alive. I know when to quit while I'm ahead."

I didn't know what to say. That was my grandpa he was talking about. I felt an unreasoning rage against the dumb ass Joely Swinburne.

And then against Noni.

The Schneider was making nuzzly moves towards me. I let him do it. That much he was allowed. And he'd earned it, if only with the price of pain.

Nuzzly nuzzly. Kissy kiss.

"Goodbye, Noni."

"Goodbye, Sam."

Sadie was bound to ask me if I'd kissed anyone while I was away. I hoped this didn't count.

He was in the car now. The engine started. I saw him wave and raised my hand to wave back. Noni would have made with a handkerchief and looked perfect. I had a handkerchief somewhere, but now wasn't the time to start fumbling in my clothes. He might get the wrong idea and tell the driver to stop and bring him back.

189

"Goodbye!"

In a moment's inspiration I blew him a kiss.

Take that, Schneider. Thus perish all who mess with the womenfolk of Zachary Waters.

The car disappeared behind a row of blossoming hedges. I stood, staring after it for a long moment, my last moment of relative freedom before I had to go back inside and face the music. Beyond the garden, beyond the fence, the desert beckoned. Maybe I should just walk away into it, never to be seen again. Even in these shoes it seemed a suddenly attractive prospect.

I sighed and turned back to the house.

What was I going to say to Noni?

"Kill me now"?

How about that for starters?

LOCATION: PALM DESERT
TIME: ABOUT TWO MINUTES POST-SCHNEIDER DISASTER, ABOUT ONE MINUTE PRE-NONI APOCALYPSE

Sara was standing in the hall, looking anxious.

"How is she?" I asked.

"She's not very happy."

I guessed that was something of an understatement.

I walked slowly up the stairs and paused outside Noni's door. As I predicted, now Sam Schneider had gone, the volume had been racked right back up. All for my benefit. I took several deep breaths and walked in.

I knew I had to face the music. What I hadn't quite expected was for it to be on such an operatic scale. It was like stumbling into the trombone section during one of Wagner's more dramatic episodes.

Noni was writhing on the pillows, howling like a

beast in torment (rather like Sam's performance on the sofa not so very long before). Sándor was sitting in the corner, his arms folded on his chest, looking daggers. Alec was standing by the bed looking exasperated. As I came in, I thought I heard him say, "Pull yourself together, woman." There was no sign of Esteban. He was probably outside hosing what remained of the Schneider manhood off the tiles and into the rose bed.

I stood for a minute, not knowing what to do or say. I had been planning on grovelling apologies and endless pretty tears, but now, after that last conversation with Sam Schneider about Noni and Grandpa Zack, I wasn't sure I was feeling quite so guilt-stricken.

Noni spotted me at last, in between howls. The siren shut off, the seizures ceased with remarkable abruptness and she shot up into a sitting position.

"How could you?" Her voice rang with accusation.

I was about to launch into some rambling excuse, but I didn't get a chance to answer.

"Sara told me all about it. You stabbed him with a fork! And then, to make matters worse, you started fooling around on that appalling skateboard and ... I can't even bring myself to repeat what you did with that. As if it hadn't caused enough damage already!"

Whatever happened to "Skateboards don't kill people; people kill people"?

"It vas not her fault!"

This came from Sándor. Hey, I'd thought he was glowering at me, but no, Noni was getting the full benefit of the Keczkes disapproval. That cheered me up a bit.

"He was groping my leg," I said. "And then he grabbed my bum."

191

"He did?"

It was her turn to cheer up. A disgusting gleam of excitement and gratification flickered across her face before she reverted to wounded heroine mode.

"Yes, he did! It was gross."

"That was no reason to stab him with your fork!"

Excuse me, but I thought that gave me every reason to do precisely that. And worse.

"I didn't realize it was him when I stabbed him."

"What do you mean you didn't know it was him? Sándor was listening at the window. He heard every word."

I explained.

I heard Alec give a snort of suppressed laughter. Noni looked unimpressed.

"And what about the skateboard?"

What about the skateboard? She knew what had happened. I remained mulishly silent.

Noni sank back as if exhausted and closed her eyes.

"I asked you to do this one thing for me. Just one thing. It meant so much to me. You knew that! And you ... you..." She produced a handkerchief (how come she always had them right there whenever she needed one?) and began to sob into it like a professional mourner.

This was going too far.

"Well, I'm sorry, I'm sure," I said. "I did my best. I'm sorry it wasn't good enough. And it wasn't just one thing. I've had days and days of it. And it's been awful! But even then it wouldn't have been so bad if Sam Schneider had kept his hairy hands to himself. You knew what he was like! I know you did. But it didn't stop you, did it? It didn't stop you dressing me up and sending me out there on my own to spend the day in the company of a serial groper!" I was shouting now. "And it was all your own fault. If you didn't drink the way you do, none of this would have happened, would it? He was right. Sam Schneider was right. You never should have left Grandpa Zack for that dumb ass whatever his name was. Grandpa Zack wouldn't have let you do this. He would never make me do anything like this. But that's because he's a real person who cares about other people, especially other people he loves. He even still cares about you. He must be mad!"

I had begun to tear off the Noni trappings by now. I hurled the hat to the floor and ripped that loathsome scarf off my head. Sara sprang forward to help me as I began to fumble for the zip in the back of the dress.

"You don't care about anyone but yourself! That's your trouble. Well, I blew it. The movie's off. And you know what? I don't care."

I stormed to the door.

"I want to go home," I said. "I never wanted to come here anyway. I don't care if Mom and Dad are away. I can stay with my friend Sadie. And I can see all my other friends as well. Friends, Noni! People my own age."

I realized I was still wearing the sling-backs. I took them off and balanced one in each hand.

"This is like living in an asylum for aging lunatics! You're all nuts. Even Sándor. Even Sara. Esteban too. But only because they put up with you! Well, I won't any more. I've had it! Good-bye, Noni. GOOD..."

Zing! There went the first sling-back, just grazing her ear.

"... BYE!"

And there went the other.

I think that one was a direct hit.

193

Then I stormed out, slamming the door so hard behind me it bounced straight open again. Which is probably why I was still able to hear Alec say "Chuffing Nora! She is so like you, it's unreal!" Then I slammed my own bedroom door, only this time I made sure it stayed shut.

LOCATION: PALM DESERT, MY ROOM, AKA "SANCTUARY"
TIME: TIME TO CALM DOWN

I called Grandpa Zack.

He was the only one I could talk to about what I'd been through. He was the only one who would understand.

He did.

He also went absolutely mental. I've never heard him so mad. He yelled and cussed and called Sam Schneider every name under the sun. Which I thought was a bit harsh. In fairness, the guy didn't know it wasn't Noni he was groping (Groping Grandma – wasn't that the title of the movie?) but her fifteen-year-old granddaughter who'd never even snogged anyone before and had no boobs.

Then he started on Noni.

I've heard Grandpa Zack cussing before, but even I was impressed at what he could come out with when he really spat on his hands and got down to it. "Horse feathers! That woman has horse feathers for brains!" I actually had to hold the phone away from my ear. The funny thing was, the madder he got, the more I calmed down. I was beginning to feel a bit bad about all those awful things I'd said to Noni. OK, I'd meant them at the time, but now, as Grandpa Zack raged on –

"... letting you anywhere near that pervert, Schneider!" – I thought I'd gone a bit too far.

"Put her on!"

What?

I hadn't been paying proper attention during the last tirade and this brought me up short.

"What do you mean?"

"Get Noni! I want to talk to her. I'll give her a piece of my mind."

"No! You mustn't!"

"Get her on the phone!"

"No, really Grandpa, I don't think that's a good idea."

"It's the best idea I've had all day!"

"No, please, I really don't want to have to deal with her right now. I kind of lost of my temper with her."

That made him stop.

"You did? Good for you. D'you tell her what you thought of her?"

"Yes, I did. And ... er ... I threw my shoes at her."

"D'you hit her?"

"I think so."

"Terrific! That's my girl!"

I could hardly tell him that at the moment I'd thrown the shoes I hadn't been his girl at all. I'd been Noni.

"What am I going to do? Can't I come stay with you? How's the hip?"

"The hip's doing just great. I'm getting about on a couple of sticks now. You'd laugh if you saw me."

Somehow I didn't think I would. More like burst into tears of relief.

"So can I come?"

I heard him sigh.

"You know I'd love to have you," he said. "Anything to get you out of that madhouse. But you have to talk to Noni first. You can't just storm out in a huff."

He was right. All those things I'd said. I had to try and make peace with her somehow.

"I feel kind of bad now. Maybe I should stay."

"Whatever you think is best, chicken. But no more dressing up nonsense. She's gotta cut that out."

"There's no need," I said. "Sam Schneider won't be back. Even if he wanted to, he'd be too scared of what I might do next."

Grandpa Zack made a harrumphing noise into the phone.

"Tell me again what happened with the skate-board."

I told him. Again. This time he laughed. Hard. And for a long time.

"Ain't you something," he said at last. "You Waters women. You are something else."

"That's funny," I said. "Sam Schneider said almost the same thing. And I'll tell you something else he said. He said Noni should never have left you. He said you were the only man who knew how to handle her."

"He said that?"

"Yup."

"Well, I'll be darned. Sam Schneider said that? The son of a gun!"

He sounded pleased.

"I should go," I said. "I miss you. I wish you were here. You'd know what to do."

"I miss you too, chicken. Hey – are you crying?"

"No."

Yes.

"I'm fine."

Sniff.

"I love you."

"Love you too."

"Remember what I said. Don't stand any nonsense."

It was a bit late for that now.

"I won't, Grandpa. Bye for now. I'll call again soon."

"You do that."

He put the phone down. Just in time. The tears I could cope with, but now my nose was starting to run.

Sometimes a good cry is exactly what you need. I dove my face into the pillows and wailed my heart out for what felt like hours. At last I calmed down enough to roll onto my back gulping and sniffing. My face was throbbing. I was hot and my eyes and nose felt like they'd swelled like balloons. I am definitely not one of those people who can cry and still look attractive. Not that I was much to write home about even at my best. I dragged myself off the bed and into the bathroom to inspect the damage.

Whoa! I looked like a hamster. My nose was a bright pink blob and my cheeks appeared to be stuffed with hazelnuts or whatever hamsters like to pack in there in times of stress. And I'd conveniently forgotten about the make-up. It was everywhere. Just how much mascara could two sets of eyelashes take? Clean-up time.

As I finally stepped out of the shower, I thought I heard the phone.

Oh no. I hoped it wasn't Grandpa Zack calling to bawl Noni out after all. I still wasn't sure what I was going to say to her, and if she'd just been hauled over the coals by ex-husband number two, I didn't think it was likely to improve her mood.

I'd wrapped myself in a towel and was trying to detangle my hair when there was a knock at the bathroom door.

Not Noni, surely?

I opened it a crack and peered round.

It was Sara.

She wasn't looking any less anxious than when I saw her last.

Now what?

"Sam Schneider's on the phone. He's asking to talk to Noni. Should I let her take it, or do you want to speak to him?"

Sam Schneider? What did he want now? Probably to sue Noni for assault.

"I'd better take it," I said. "Can you put him through up here?"

"Sure."

Sara picked up the phone by my bed and did something clever with the buttons.

"Hello, Mr Schneider, I have Miss Waters for you."

She crossed the room holding it out to me.

"Hello, Sam?"

Sara waggled her eyebrows and tiptoed out.

"Noni!"

He sounded cheerful enough. And his voice had obviously returned to normal. Maybe he wasn't going to sue me after all.

"How are you doing, Sam?"

He laughed.

(He laughed?)

"I'm fine. Full recovery. Takes more than a kick in the pants to keep me down."

I'd bear that in mind. If I ever met him again, I'd

make sure I was armed with more than a fork and whatever else came to hand.

"I'm glad to hear it. I'm so sorry…"

"Stop it! I don't want to hear any more about it."

Fine by me.

"I'm glad you called," I said. "I've been worried. Thanks for letting me know you're OK."

"No problemo. But that's not the main reason I was calling."

He was going to sue me.

"What with one thing and another" – the one thing being the fork, the other being the skateboard, I guessed – "we never did get to talk about the movie."

"Er … no."

At least he was trying to break it to me gently. Not that the inevitable "thanks, but no thanks, Noni" was exactly going to come as a shock.

"We need to talk to Jack Winemaker. Then you can talk to your agent. You still have an agent, don't you? It's relatively early days yet, but once we know you're on board, we can move forward with the rest of the casting."

"You mean, you still want me to make the picture?"

"Of course I do." He sounded surprised. "You are interested, aren't you? I got the impression you were right up for it last we spoke."

"Er … yes! Sure! I just thought…"

"You thought what? Whatever it was, stop thinking it right now. What I need to hear from you now is 'Yes, Sam, I'm up for the picture.'"

"Yes, Sam, I'm up for the picture."

"Good girl. Listen, I gotta run now. Jack Winemaker's waiting to hear from me. He's going to be real pleased about this. I'll be in touch, OK."

"OK."

OK!

"Bye, Noni."

"Bye, Sam."

This time I had the handkerchief right there, but a) it was soaking wet, and b) he wouldn't have seen it anyway.

Sara was waiting outside on the landing, still looking anxious. It was getting to be a habit.

"He wants Noni to make the picture," I said.

"He does?"

"That's what he said."

"You mean, even after…" OK, OK, no need to rub it in. "We'd better go tell her."

I liked the "we".

"Can you do it?"

"No! It has to come from you. Don't worry. She isn't really mad with you. She gets like that and then it all blows over."

She smiled.

"Hey," she said. "You did it. Well done!"

I had! I really had! At last it was starting to sink in.

"I can hardly believe it," I said. "I mean, the awful things I did to that poor guy."

Sara shrugged.

"I guess some men like it when you treat them rough," she said.

If I thought I looked bad, Noni looked terrible. She was lying, eyes closed, with her face turned into the pillows.

"Er … Noni?" I said nervously.

"Go away! You've broken my heart."

I looked at Sara, appalled, but she just shook her head and waved at me to carry on.

"I've got something to tell you."

"I think you've said everything I need to hear."

Touchy touchy.

"No," I said. "This is new. I just came off the phone from Sam Schneider."

The eyes opened.

Aha!

"That was very decent of him to call. I hope you told him how very sorry you are."

Don't you mean, how very sorry *you* are?

"Of course I did. But that's not why he called."

"Oh?"

Definite interest now.

"He wants you to be in the movie."

She sat up so quickly I jumped back in alarm.

"He does?"

Now I had a proper view of her I could see she had a nice new Band-aid on the side of her forehead. Another shining example of Sara's wound management skills. So I had made contact with that second shoe. Good.

She looked like she'd been crying too. Not so hamsterish as me, but the signs were all there. At least this should cheer her up.

"He does. He'll be calling back to set up a meeting with Jack Winemaker. He says you should contact your agent."

She paused to think about this. Then she actually smiled. I felt several little knots come undone inside me.

"We did it!" she said. "We did it!"

There it was again. What was with this "we" business? But this wasn't a time to be ungracious.

201

"We did," I said.

Now she looked at me properly.

"You've been crying," she said. She made it sound like a crime. "You look awful."

Not that she was exactly a basket of fruit herself right now.

"So have you," I said.

"No, I haven't."

Have so!

"Look," I said. "It's been quite a day for all of us. And I'm exhausted. I said a lot of things I didn't mean, and I'm sorry. But it's turned out OK now, so can we just put everything aside and start again?"

I thought she was going to start pouting, but instead her face went all wobbly. She didn't actually cry right there in front of me, but it was obviously touch and go.

"Yes," she said when she'd got control of her lips again. "I'd appreciate that very much, darling."

Hey, I was "darling" again!

"And I'd like to do something for you. Some treat to show you how grateful I am for everything you've done. And that includes coming out here to spend your summer with a tiresome old lady when you could have been at home with your friends."

Enough already with the guilt!

"You don't have to do that," I said. "But there is one thing I would like."

"Anything, darling. What is it?"

I told her about my date with Lucas and the skaters at the mall. She obviously thought it was kind of a weird request, but she said I could go.

Well, she could hardly refuse now. Could she?

\* \* \*

It felt great to be me again: Kat. The Kat with no hat. Kat
with no dress, no stockings, no heels. Kat in trousers. Kat
in sandals. Kat in the Axe-baby T-shirt. Kat swooping up
and down the mall car park on her skateboard with a
group of like-minded teenagers. Esteban had gone to
fetch us all cold drinks, taking Madge, who for some reason had made a fuss when we were leaving the house and
had been allowed to come along.

Lucas was showing me how to do that trick properly. It was easy when you'd practised it. And you were
wearing the right gear. It was all about balance. I was
doing it now: jump, twist, land, swivel, kick. No oops!
this time. Esteban reappeared with a bag of cold cans
and we took a break.

I'd just about finished my drink when I heard a
squeal of tyres and a powder-blue Cadillac shot
through the entrance barrier and into the car park.

"Look at that," said Lucas. "That guy's going way
too fast. That's how people get hurt."

I didn't answer. Surely I'd seen that car somewhere
before.

It careered towards us. Esteban was already halfway
to meet it. I jumped to my feet. What was this? Sam
Schneider's hired assassin? A drive-by shooting?

Alec's ginger head appeared out of the driver's window. His face was even redder than usual. I scampered
up behind Esteban.

"What's up?"

"Sam Schneider's turned up at the house again."

"What? But he can't…"

"And he's expecting Jack Winemaker to join him soon. Girl, you're on again."

I didn't ask questions. No point. Esteban was practical as ever.

"Where's Noni?"

"She's in her room lying low. Thank God you took Madge. We told him Noni was out with you, but we expected her back any time."

"OK, but how are we going to get Kat into the house to change without him seeing?"

"We're not going to try. I've brought everything with me. What we have to figure out is where I can help her change."

My mind was bouncing about in my skull. A voice somewhere near the front of it was screaming: "No-o-o! Not again!" But I hadn't completely lost my wits.

"We can go to Rick's," I said. "Those changing cubicles are big enough for two of us."

Even when one of them is you.

Esteban jerked a thumb at him.

"You get out and go with her," he said. "I'll park the car."

Seconds counted. Do you have any idea how long it takes for false nail adhesive to dry?

I bid a fond farewell to the guys and told them an unexpected family friend had turned up and I had to go home, which was more or less true. They asked if I'd be able to come back again any time, and I said I thought I would. Add it to Noni's account in Kat's Little of Book of Favours Owed. They seemed impressed by Alec. He was carrying his case, he had a garment bag over one arm, a hatbox looped over his wrist and another bag dangling from his fingers that screamed "Shoes". He looked like a walking clothes horse. I took the hatbox and the shoe bag and we cantered into the mall.

We hit Rick's Place like a tropical storm: Hurricane Noni. This time Rick was home. He opened his mouth to launch into the usual aria of joy and welcome, but we hurtled past him with a brief "Hi there!" and disappeared into one of the changing cubicles at the back. Alec hooked up the garment bag and unzipped the dress Sara had chosen. Not the backless pink jobby, I was glad to see, but the white one with red poppies I had been wearing for the upside-down ice cube humiliation event. It seemed to have recovered better than I had. Out came the undies, the scarf, yesterday's hat. Yesterday's hat? I didn't want to be seen wearing the same hat twice! Then the sandals. Alec dropped them onto the floor in the corner.

"I'll let you change. If you need any help, shout. I'll be right outside."

I was aware that the cubicle curtain appeared to have grown a fringe. I looked at it. Hair. Moustaches. Rick, clearly overcome with curiosity, was peering under the curtain at our two sets of feet and the sandals in the corner. I think he realized he'd been spotted. The face fuzz disappeared and a voice outside said, "That is you, isn't it, Alec? Can I help you with anything in there?"

Alec winked at me.

"I'll go calm him down," he said.

The shop door buzzed open and I heard Junior fly out from behind the counter, yipping like a fiend. That must mean Esteban and Madge had arrived. I left the men to sort out their differences while I tore off my skaterwear and began to hurl myself into Noni's clothes. More haste, less speed. The first thing I did was shove a finger right through one of the stockings as I was trying to drag it on. Sara, in her infinite wisdom, had packed a spare pair. Almost whimpering with frustration I grabbed another and tried to be more careful. Then the dress.

"Zip!" I yelled.

Alec was there in seconds.

"Nice work," he said. "Leave the scarf until I've done your face."

He bobbed back out and reappeared with the stool and the dreaded case.

"Hop up on here and keep still," he said.

"How's Rick?"

Totally gobsmacked," he said. "And more excited than a basket of puppies."

Talk about a two-minute make-over. We must have broken the land speed record for applying mascara. (Note the "we".) Then he swiped my hair with a brush – "Ow!" – and muffled me up in the scarf. On with the hat. Then, a touch I especially enjoyed: he knelt at my feet and strapped me into Those Sandals.

I got down off the stool and he ran a critical eye over me.

"You'll do," he said. "Out you go. I'll pack up here and catch up with you."

I pulled back the curtain and stepped out.

Rick was waiting. I was getting so used to the whole Noni-transformation thing, I didn't really think about it any more. It was new to him, though. He clapped both hands to his face and screamed like a kettle.

"Oh my sweet Lord Jesus! You doll!"

"Hi," I said, feeling awkward. "I'm sorry about this.

And thanks for letting us use your store to change."

He was already circling me like a ewe with a new-born lamb.

"Now don't you worry about that for a second, you sweet thing. It's an honour! Really! Noni Waters's granddaughter!"

"We should go," said Esteban. "Thanks, Rick."

"One thing," Rick said, his delight suddenly clouding. "The other day. When you came in with the funny little guy and bought that shirt." Ah yes, that shirt – Il Hideoso. "Was that really Noni? Or was that you?"

"It was me, I'm afraid," I said.

He let out a long, awed breath.

"But then..." His moustaches wriggled. "What about the 'Miss Noni Waters' contest? You said..."

"Oh, she'll do it," I said. "You don't need to worry about that. She'll still do it. And that's a promise."

"Oh thank you, thank you," he breathed. "This year I have high hopes that Taylor will win. He's my other half. You met him in here the other day. He does your pool."

Pool God?

Rick and Pool God were an item?

Pool God was gay?

A whole magical world crumbled around me. I reeled. I think I may have clutched at the counter. Alec gave me a funny look. I toyed with the idea of slumping to the floor and moaning. Pool God! My nearest, dearest fantasy! The one bright and beautiful light in what had been a wilderness of gloom. And he was gay? Life was so unfair. Life was beyond unfair. How many hours had I wasted dreaming about him, fretting that I had no boobs? And he didn't even care. He probably hadn't even noticed. Aaargh! I closed my eyes for a moment and allowed myself one final, fleeting vision of him: standing by the pool, bronzed and beautiful, all tan, teeth and triceps. I know I whimpered. I hoped Rick thought it was Madge.

Then the weakness passed. I could be strong. So what did it matter if my heart was broken? There were people out there waiting to see Noni Waters. *The* Noni Waters. And I wasn't about to disappoint them. As I stepped delicately out from amidst the rubble of my shattered dreams, I strapped on my bravest smile. I was Noni Waters now.

"I'll put in a good word for him," I said. Then, to show there were no hard feelings, I added, "He does have lovely legs."

Rick clasped my fingers and bent over them, clearly moved. But not as moved as I was when I looked down and saw my hands.

"Nails!" I screeched. "We forgot the nails!"

I don't know if you've ever tried sticking on a full set of false nails in the back of a speeding Jaguar, but all I can tell you is don't try it if you can possibly avoid it. We left the blue Caddy at the mall, so Alec could come along and perform this essential task on the way back to the house. I don't know what the skater guys thought when Esteban and Alec reappeared in the car park, not with the girl they'd disappeared with less than twenty minutes before, but with the aging glam queen from two days ago who had claimed to be Grandma. An aging glam queen, moreover, who was putting on a surprising turn of speed and shrieking, "How could you forget the nails!" at the harassed looking giant who owned the Cadillac. I even forgot myself enough to wave, which really threw them.

208

"Watch the car," I shouted. "The blue one. We'll be back for it later."

When the bloodbath *chez* Noni was over.

I leant back against the seat while Alec cursed and tried to unstick my little finger nail from the inside of his wrist, and attempted to imagine what I could possibly do to Sam Schneider this time.

And, of course, there was Jack Winemaker to worry about.

No doubt I should be planning something especially deadly for him.

I closed my eyes and moaned softly.

It didn't matter. Nothing mattered any more.

Pool God was gay.

Life had lost all meaning.

LOCATION: PALM DESERT
TIME: TWO MINUTES TO LIFT-OFF – AGAIN

As soon as we were through the gates Esteban slowed right down. No need to arrive looking as hysterical as we felt. Sara had the front door open before we'd even stopped. Alec ducked down in the back, and when Esteban opened the car door for me I gathered up Madge and swung my legs out, ankles together, as gracefully as I'd been taught. Time for yet another entrance. I was getting so used to them by now I was beginning to wonder if I'd ever be able to walk into a room naturally again. Two days back at school in full uniform (the one apparently designed by short-sighted, colour-blind nuns) should sort that one out.

"He's drinking coffee by the pool," Sara whispered. Don't ask me why she was whispering. He would have needed the hearing of a bat to pick up what we were saying out here.

"Any sign of Jack Winemaker?"

"Not yet."

"Where's Noni?"

"Last I saw she'd shut herself in the bathroom and was having hysterics. I left Sándor trying to persuade her to open the door."

Oh great. That was really going to help my concentration.

"How did she get in there?"

"Crutches."

Even better. Now Noni was semi-mobile. I could only hope Sándor's powers of persuasion were not up to the task and she stayed right where she was. Hysterics were fine – she could have sixteen fits for all I cared. So long as she was quiet.

Esteban was looking back over the desert, shading his eyes.

"There's another car on the road," he said. Maybe heading this way. It could be Jack Winemaker. Hard to tell. But it won't be here for another ten, fifteen minutes, even if it is. You'd better get inside and see Mr Schneider."

Sam Schneider sprang up as soon as I appeared and rushed over for the whole huggy-kissy routine. I submitted to it with good grace, especially as he seemed a lot less keen on frisking me for concealed weapons than he had last time. Maybe the skateboard had taught him a lesson. I murmured surprise and delight, and apologized for being out when he arrived.

"I should have called," he said. "But I managed to get hold of Jack this morning to tell him the good news, and he said he was heading out here on other business today, so I said, 'Hey, how about you and me go and talk through the new picture with Noni first?' – by the way he's thrilled that you'll do it – and he said 'Sure' so I said 'I'm going over there now, how about you join us?'"

He snapped his knuckles.

"Bada-bing, bada-boom!" he concluded, as though this made everything perfectly clear.

"How absolutely wonderful" I said. "I'm so delighted!"

Amazing how I could tell such appalling lies and not be struck dead at his feet.

"But – no more skateboards!"

I gave a careless and merry laugh.

"It's gone," I said.

"Come, sit down with me. I was having coffee."

"Sara's bringing me some iced tea," I said. I'd also handed Madge over to her for protective custody. The last thing I wanted was for that pint-sized piece of fur and attitude to try for a rematch with the Schneider ankles.

"Now," he said when we were both settled at the table (which I swear we both checked instinctively for lurking forks). "We need to talk figures. Fees."

Did we? I couldn't do this. If he wanted to know how many million Noni was worth he was talking to the wrong woman. Yesterday, I would have given her away free to anyone who'd take her out of my life, and then offered them that fifty bucks I still had to pay for the removal.

"Shouldn't you be talking to my agent about that?" I guessed.

I saw his eyes narrow.

"Well, yes, but ... before I do, I thought we could float a few numbers."

Two could play at that game. I smelled more rat than in *Wind in the Willows*. I narrowed my own eyes behind the sunglasses.

"I don't think so," I said firmly. "You really will have to talk to ... to..." A name? A name? Give me a name. Who was Noni's agent anyway? Was it a him or a her? "... to them about it."

He took my hand, but this time in a respectful rather than a grabby sort of a way.

I heard the doorbell ring. That would be Jack Winemaker. Good. Just in time to stop Schneider pulling any more funny business.

What was I saying? I meant – bad! Now I had to cope with someone else who'd known Noni since the dawn of time. I resisted the temptation to turn and stare. Instead I swallowed a shudder and put my own hand on top of his.

"Now, now," I said. I suspected Noni would have said "You naughty man", but there were limits. I may have been wearing whisper-thin support hose, but I still had some standards.

I was aware of the fountainarium door sliding open.

"That will be Jack now," I said and wondered why Sam's jaw had suddenly dropped open.

I turned, plastering on that all purpose Noni-smile just in time to catch my new visitor at full bellow.

"Noni! Schneider – you pervert! Get your hands off each other. I might have known!"

It was Grandpa Zack.

How the table didn't go over this time, I shall never know. Both Sam Schneider and I shot to our feet with a well-coordinated yelp of alarm.

"Grandpa Zack!" I said.

"Who?" said Sam, then peered more closely. "Hey, you're that Zachary Waters fellow, ain't you? Used to be married to Noni. What the hell are you doing here?"

"I could ask you the same thing," growled Grandpa Zack. He looked thinner than usual, and he was leaning on a couple of sticks. "Except I know damn fine why you're here. Noni! Where's my granddaughter?"

I stared at him.

"She's ... er ... she's..."

"She's with friends in Hawaii," said Sam. "Isn't she?"

He looked at me.

"The hell she is!" snapped Grandpa Zack. "I spoke to her in this house only yesterday. Where is she, Noni? What have you done with her?"

Speech failed me. I waved my arms helplessly.

"I'm going to find her, and I'm going to take her home with me! Treatin' her the way you have. Dressin' her up and passin' her off as you! Have you no shame, woman?"

He was really kicking into his stride now. I was aware Sam Schneider was looking at me.

"Will somebody please tell me what this guy is talking about?" he said.

Esteban appeared.

"Excuse me, sir," he said. And then he stopped and goggled.

"Esteban!"

"Mr Waters?"

"Yup. I remember you. Surprised to find a sensible man like you still working in a crazy farm like this. Where's Kat?"

Esteban looked across at me. I shook my head as imperceptibly as possible.

"Er … I don't know right now, sir. What I wanted to ask you was what I should do about the dog. Can I let him out of the crate?"

"Sure you can. Take him to the kitchen. Give him something to eat and drink. Poor animal's been stuck in there for hours. Damn airline wouldn't let me take him in the cabin with me."

Spud?

Esteban disappeared.

"You brought Spud?"

He didn't seem to find the question odd.

"Had to. Couldn't get anyone to take him at such short notice. Got the first flight this morning. Had to box him up."

"Will somebody please tell me what's going on?" Sam Schneider was beginning to sound desperate now.

There was a scrabbling of claws and a large white shape barrelled out through the open door barking at the top of its lungs. Spud had got away from Esteban.

"Spud!" shouted Grandpa Zack.

"Spud!" I yelled.

"Jesus Christ!" shouted Sam Schneider and jumped onto the table.

Then it collapsed.

Spud shot past Grandpa Zack, who made a hopeless attempt to grab him but only succeeded in dropping one of his sticks. He gave a single bark of joyous recognition and threw himself into my arms.

I fell down. Of course. We're talking seriously heavy dog here. But I didn't care. I rolled around on the ground hugging him and crying and calling his name while he licked my face as if all that awful make-up was the best thing he'd ever tasted in the world. I was aware of Sam Schneider sitting near me, rubbing his elbows and cursing and trying to shift away from the flailing arms and legs and waggling tail that seemed to be filling the whole garden.

Grandpa Zack recovered his stick and hobbled over.

"Get down, Spud" he shouted, prodding him in the ribs. "Leave her alone. You haven't even been introduced!"

It had no effect. I managed to push him away long enough to gasp. "It's OK!" and sat up. My hat had come off, the sunglasses were hanging from my ear by one leg and my scarf had unwrapped itself and was halfway down my back. My stockings were in shreds.

Grandpa Zack looked at me and frowned. He bent forward.

"Noni?"

"Zachary Waters!"

The voice seemed to come from nowhere. We looked round.

"Whatever possessed you to come here and bring that dog?!"

We looked up.

Noni was standing on the roof terrace, waving an angry crutch at the scene below.

"Noni!" – Grandpa Zack

"Noni?" – Sam Schneider.

"Noni." – Me, very quietly, with my eyes closed.

Sara came out of the house.

"Mr Winemaker is here," she said.

And Madge shot out from behind her.

Then all hell really did break loose.

\* \* \*

She took one look at Spud and went for him like a guided missile. I threw myself to one side on top of Sam Schneider, who fell over backwards again. I heard Spud give a single yip of surprise and then a howl of pain. Somewhere in the background Grandpa Zack and Noni were also at it hammer and tongs. I scrambled onto all fours and struggled to my feet. Then I gave Sam Schneider a hand and hauled him up too. Spud was racing round the pool, yowling, pursued by the ever-feisty Madge, who was hurling herself at him, snapping and shrieking.

Sara and a man I'd never seen before were standing in the doorway watching the whole circus in action.

Sam Schneider brushed himself down and looked at me.

"Noni?" he said. Then he looked up at the figure on the roof who had given up on expressing herself with the crutches and was now relying on the power of the voice alone. "Noni?"

Then he looked back at me.

"You're not Noni."

I shook my head.

He took a minute to think about this. Enough time for Spud and Madge to start on their second lap.

"Who are you, then?"

"I'm Kat."

"Kat?"

"Noni's granddaughter."

"So you're not in Hawaii?"

Another shake of the head.

"How old are you?"

"Fifteen."

He reeled. I thought for a minute he was going to sit back down again.

"Jeezus!" he said, and put his head in his hands.

"I think we should go inside," I said. "It's kind of noisy out here."

At which point Spud, driven to the point of madness by the persistent and valiant Madge, hurled himself into the pool.

We all gathered in Noni's room: me, Grandpa Zack, Sam Schneider, Jack Winemaker, Sándor and Alec. Esteban and Sara were downstairs sorting out the dogs.

Noni was trying to explain. It wasn't going too well.

"I can't believe you would do this," Sam Schneider was saying.

"Totally irresponsible!" Grandpa Zack was grumbling.

I began to feel sorry for her.

"Look," I said. "Give her a break! It was my idea, after all."

Now they all looked at me. I had changed into my own clothes by now and washed my face.

"Your idea?" – Sam Schneider.

"Yes, kind of. Noni hurt her ankle and didn't want you to know."

He looked at her.

"How d'you hurt your ankle?" he said, suspiciously.

"Um," was all Noni managed.

"She fell off my skateboard," I said. "That was my fault too."

"That goddam skateboard!" he snarled.

"It was my idea to find a double. I just didn't think it would be me."

"You made her do this!" shouted Grandpa Zack.

"No, she didn't. Not really," I said. "I could have said 'no'."

Which was also kind of true.

Jack Winemaker spoke. It was the first time he'd really contributed anything since he'd arrived. I think he'd been too stunned.

"Well, I hate to rain on your parade," he said. "But I have bad news."

Now we all looked at him.

"The movie's off."

There was an outbreak of exclamations and questions from around the room.

"I'm sorry, Sam. I got a call from the backers an hour ago. They're pulling out."

"They are? Why?"

"They got a hostile take-over bid from one of the major studios this morning. I can't name names here. I'll tell you about it when we're back in LA."

"We can find new backers!"

"Possibly. But for now, it's off."

Noni gave a little wail. I was amazed to see Grandpa Zack go over to the bed and take her hand.

"You mean we went through all this for nothing?" This was Alec.

"You mean *I* went through all this for nothing," I said.

"Sorry," said Jack Winemaker.

"Hell, no!" said Sam Schneider. "We'll make a different picture. A better picture. How about this? Listen. This is a great story. You take a movie star. She's been in a lot of pictures, but she's retired. Then she gets the chance to make another picture again, but she's ill. She's bedridden. So she gets her granddaughter who looks just like her to take her place. Neat, huh? Is that a good storyline or what? Can't you just see that? Starring Noni Waters. Imagine that. Another Noni Waters picture."

218

He had leaped to his feet and was pacing round the room excitedly.

"And who gets to play the granddaughter?" Jack Winemaker asked.

Sam pointed a finger.

"She does, of course."

What?

"Yes!" shouted Noni.

"No!" shouted Grandpa Zack.

"Brilliant," said Alec.

"Perfect," said Sándor

"You're all nuts," I said.

"And what will you call this movie?" said Jack Winemaker with a wry smile.

"*A Goddess Returns,*" said Noni.

"There won't be any damn movie," said Grandpa Zack.

"*Your Face, My Face,*" offered Alec.

"*Ze Power of ze Vill,*" Sándor suggested smugly.

"I can't believe you," I said. "You're all crazy. You should hear yourselves. You're like a big bunch of kids. I thought this was supposed to be a serious business. Why don't you all act your age?"

"That's it!" shouted Sam Schneider. "That's perfect!"

"What is?" I said.

"The name of the movie: *Act Your Age.* What do you think?"

But I had already gone.

Somewhere in the house there was a big wet dog that needed my attention. And a little white one.

I needed the company of rational beings.

I found them in the kitchen. Spud had his nose in a

huge bowl of food and Madge was sitting next to him, looking on, wagging her tail.

"Hey! They made friends," I said.

"Yeah," said Esteban. "Madge thought he was attacking you out there. That was the problem."

"You did, Madge? You took on the mighty Spud for me? What a girl."

She didn't even look at me. She only had eyes for Spud.

"Do you have their leads?" I said. "I'm going to take them for a walk. Open the gates. I think it needs to be a long one."

"What about the others?"

"Leave them to it," I said. "Right now I want to be alone. No more picture talk. Just me, the dogs and the open highway. Like *Easy Rider*, only with fewer Harleys and more Chihuahuas."

"Good idea," said Esteban. "But you could take your skateboard."

What a man.

I took the lead and snapped it onto Spud's collar. Madge was already set.

"What do I tell them when they find you've gone?"

I just smiled at him.

"You'll think of something," I said.

LOCATION: A PARK IN NORTH OXFORD
TIME: THREE WEEKS LATER

Jamie and I were sitting on a bench with our skateboards. Right now we were taking a break. Sadie was off shopping for a new personality somewhere in town. I think she'd heard they were on offer at Superdrug. It was just him and me.

220

We were talking about the summer.

"I still can't believe your grandmother's a movie star," he was saying.

He still had that floppy blond look that hung over one eye. Cute. OK, so he wasn't Pool God, but then, would I want him to be?

"Yeah," I said. "We don't talk about it much. It's a bit like admitting to a streak of insanity in the family."

"I don't get it. I think it'd be cool to have someone famous related to you."

"It's OK," I said. "But it can get a bit tiresome."

"What about your granddad?"

Grandpa Zack? Last I'd seen of him, he and Noni were standing holding hands, waving me off at the airport. Or maybe they were holding each other up. Neither of them was any too steady on their pins.

"He's cool," I said. "I hope you get to meet him sometime."

"I'd like that."

"Sadie said you've been offered a part in a film."

I groaned inwardly.

Sadie would. I wish I'd never let that one slip out. Might as well have told the town crier to polish up his bell.

"Yeah, well, it was just an idea. I don't think it's really going to happen."

"Would you do it?"

I shrugged.

"I don't know," I said. "I don't think I'm cut out for that sort of thing."

"You don't? Why not? I do. You were great in the play, remember."

I was aware his hand had suddenly moved closer to mine on the bench.

"You're only saying that," I said, trying not to stare. "Let's face it. I looked like an eejit."

"No, you didn't," he said. "I mean it. Really. You were so funny as that guy. I wouldn't ever dare do anything like that, especially not dressed up as a woman. I thought you were really brave."

"You made fun of my beard."

"Of course I did!" His fingers were touching mine now. "It was funny. It was supposed to be funny."

True. But I was more interested in the fingers now.

"So, why don't you do that film? It would be so cool. I'd like that. Having a girlfriend who was a movie star."

!!!!!!!!!!!!!!!!
???????????
!!!!!!!!!!!!!!!!

I looked at him.

"Did you just say what I think you said?"

He smiled.

I wanted to say "But I have no boobs."

I didn't.

Instead I thought of what Noni would do.

He looked so adorable – kind of worried too, like he'd just said the wrong thing and was about to die. And he was holding my hand properly now: gently, but firmly. Like it belonged there.

It was too much.

I kissed him. I simply had to.

I did. I really did.

And he kissed me back.

It was just like the movies.

Only a million times better.

"I'll think about it," I said, when he'd stopped. Then, seeing the look on his face, I said, "About the movie, I mean. Not the girlfriend bit. I don't need to think about that."

He smiled. He had a lovely smile.

"So now what?" he said.

"You should kiss me again," I said. "Then we move to a slow fade-out and the credits roll."

"You're the director," he said. "You get to say 'cut.'"

"Not yet," I said. "Not for a long time yet. Now, kiss me again."

And, like the superstar he was, he did.

And again.

     And again.

          And again.

               And again.

*The End*